BEST OF BINAPANI

(A Collection of Odia Short Stories in English Translation)

Selected Short Stories of Binapani Mohanty

BEST OF BINAPANI

(A Collection of Odia Short Stories in English Translation)

Selected Short Stories of Binapani Mohanty

Translated by :
Sneha Mishra

BLACK EAGLE BOOKS
Dublin, USA | Bhubaneswar, India

 Black Eagle Books
USA address:
7464 Wisdom Lane
Dublin, OH 43016

India address:
E/312, Trident Galaxy, Kalinga Nagar,
Bhubaneswar-751003, Odisha, India

E-mail: info@blackeaglebooks.org
Website: www.blackeaglebooks.org

First International Edition Published by
Black Eagle Books, 2024

BEST OF BINAPANI
Selected Short Stories of Binapani Mohanty
(A Collection of Odia Short Stories in English Translation)

Translated by : **Sneha Mishra**

Translation Copyright © Sneha Mishra

Cover & Interior Design: Ezy's Publication

ISBN- 978-1-64560-589-8 (Paperback)
Library of Congress Control Number: 2024947632

Printed in the United States of America

Dedicated to
Late Ms. Binapani Mohanty
as a humble tribute

CONTENTS

The Power and Glory of a Flood

Aparti came running to the common-yard and breathlessly to the people who were playing cards there, and to the onlookers, "How are you playing now ? Get up, get up, get up quickly. The dam is already broken for quite some time... neck-high water is rushing in."

Sanatana threw the pack of cards and said, "Hey ! just a minute ago I saw in my own eyes that the water level in the dam was waist-deep. How could the dam break ? how ? You, tell me the truth. Did someone throw something at the base-line of the dam?"

Aparti said angrily, "I cannot say this or that. Let me go home. I will go away with my children. My God ... so high was the water... my eyes could not fathom. It would have been a sin if I didn't inform you. Otherwise, I would have already gone away to my uncle's home with my children ! Well, I am going...."

The village road echoed with Aparti's breathless words, "Leave the village, water is rushing in....., leave fast, leave..."

Sanatana looked at Sukadeva's face, Sukadeva looked at Satura's, Kanduri's, Bansi's and Biju's. From yesterday, where they heard that the dam would collapse, they had been keeping a watch at the dam in turn. Last night boys guarded the whole night pitching a tent near the dam. There was no sign of any danger during the day, but inspite of the watch the dam collapsed about the last hours of the night!

Sukadeva said in an alarmed voice, "Sana ! if we knew about the leak on the dam, we could have done something. Now there is no way but to run away. Don't you remember the event that happened ten years ago."

Sanatana stood dumbfounded. He could easily visualise that event. The flood rushed violently in the midnight like a tiger. He ran upto the roof for fear of his life... With him was his wife Sundarmani... oh ! the memory of it... It was a heart-rending sight....

Seventy-five years old father and seventy years old mother. The moment he opened the door and was about to bring them outside, the flood water sucked them into its whirl. The village road was resounding with cries. No one was listening to no one – there was nothing to listen to. While climbing up the stairs to the second floor Kuna jerked himself away from Sundarmani's hands and shouted, "I am going with grandpa." Sanatana was shouting from the roof-top. But Kuna jumped into the water crying, "grandpa... grandpa...." Grandpa extended his hands to clutch Kuna. His body was not visible, only his two hands could be seen. There was no sign of mother at all ! Sundarmani was wailing holding on to Sanatana. Many of his neighbours climbed up his roof holding their children, but Sanatana's father, mother and son, Kuna were swept away in the flood in front of his very eyes in no time. He looked as far he could see holding Sundarmani tightly. The thatched houses, coconut trees, papaya trees, mango trees were all falling into the water, and swept away. There were shouting all around.

It took seven or eight days for the flood to recede. Rice and lentils which were preserved in his house in straw-bags, coconuts, pumpkins, potatoes of his garden-everything vanished. Outside and inside the home there were only neck-high deposits of mud, dirt, rubbish, and two or four decaying bodies of dogs, cows and human beings. Memory of that macabre sight rends his heart even now. Sundarmani kept sitting for seven days without taking any food-there were no more tears left in her eyes. A few food packets were dropped from the helicopter, which the children finished fighting among themselves. Sundarmani became dumb seeing that scene. She suffered from fever and cough, and finally died of pneumonia.

After that event Sanatana did not care to think of anything. He gave his lands for share-cropping. If he cooked once, he would manage with it for five days. Yet he did not suffer from pneumonia. How could he ? He was to live and to see more of this miserable world.

"Sana ! Why are you simply standing ? Water is flooding in. Cannot you hear its sound ? Where would the children go ? Yours is the only concrete house in the village. You shall have to open the door...!"

Sanatana took out the key from his waist-band and giving it said, "Take this key. Open the door and let the people stay on the roof and inside the house. Paddy, rice, potato, pumpkin-everything is there. Let me sit here. I am sitting on this common yard. You go .... I say. Don't delay..."

Sukadeva had no time. He was the headmaster of the Middle English School in the village. It was quite natural that he had some knowledge of geography. He had to save his family from the advancing flood and its all-encompassing hunger. Of course, the river was five miles away from the spot, but no one knew how fast water would rush in.

"Sir.......... Sir....... run. The water has already reached upto the lower level of the village. Let us take women and children from the school to the Master's building."

Some people addressed Sanatana as the 'Master.' His father and grandfather were zamindars. Only the concrete building, as the paternal property, now existed. It was now quite some time he donated all the lands to the Government, and a piece of land to the village school. He had laid foundation on the land which his father had gifted to Sundarmani lovingly. However small, he wanted to build a hospital after Kuna's name. But... a shower of rain fell on him. Flashes of lightning seen through the champak, bakul, wood-apple and mango trees struck fear in him. The headmasters and others had gone away. Banu came, held his arms and said, "Uncle, come, leave this place. All of them are there on your roof, and why have not you have gone there. What do I know ? come, come...."

Banu did not listen to him, he lifted him on his back and began walking. After a few minutes he started running. There were shouts, rain and lightning with thunder all around.

There was no space even for a grain left on his roof. Hari Nana who did his 'puja' in the village-temple everyday held the son of Ramu Harijan, and was trying to quiet his crying, because Ramu's wife was not to be seen anywhere in the darkness, and again Ramu had gone downstairs... the child was crying loudly as he found Hari unfamiliar to him.

Biju shouted, "who came or who did not there was no way to know. Who did such a thing ? We were all watching the dam in turn. Last night I was sitting there sleeplessly. Banu, Ramu and Nitia stood watching in the morning.... What did these loafers do in the evening... ? Bastards... they put some medicine, and broke the dam... one or two babus had come in a jeep, I have heard...."

A boy said in a trembling voice, they were looking at the dam with a torch. They have not put anything; I have seen it in my own eyes. Rather they were deeply worried."

"Shut up !" Banu said angrily. "They must have done something, I know it very well, where is Sukadeva Sir ?

"Oh ! yes, where is he ? Sukadeva might have opened the front door and the door to the staircase of Sanatana's house and... what else ? he must have rushed to fetch his wife, son and daughter from his house near the school building. After that... what ? Did the flood sweep him away or did he escape somewhere avoiding the wrath of the flood ? It was difficult to know. There are more than five hundred houses in the neighbourhood. The number of houses has increased after separations in the families. Many times, Sanatana must have told the people that if they built a stone dam there would be no fear of flood. Everybody would just hear him and then forget. There are always plans and projects for dams in this country. If a little pressure can be put on the Minister, work would start. These days the number of Government service holders has increased in the village but no one is interested to do anything about it.

Ramu ran up to the roof. He carried his wife on his back. There was a flash of lightning and all lowered their heads. The woman was stark naked, and was wailing. Sanatana untied his red towel from his waist, and threw it towards Ramu. There was no other way.

Ramu said, "Master, my wife was almost drowned in the neck-high water when I reached there. Somehow, she held on to a mango tree and was shouting helplessly. In a moment, the tree fell down; if I had not drugged her away..."

The child recognised his father's voice and cried without stop. In normal days Hari Nana, the village priest, would take a bath if he was touched even by the shadow of Ramu, because he worshipped the village-deity regularly twice a day with perfect observation of rules and rituals. He never looked at woman. If his god was well and happy, he was well and happy too !

Hari nana asked haltingly, "Ramu, what is there in the packet ?

"Some rice-flakes, lentil and rice are in this packet. The mother was bringing this for her child. The flood water took away her clothes, but could not snatch away the packet. How could Chemi hold it in her teeth I can't imagine !"

"All right, give me a little of these things. I will offer it to the deity right here. Oh Ram ! Oh Ram! In the morning when I went to offer food to the deity, I found it burnt. Then came this misery. If the deity spends the whole day without food, who would listen to our woes ?"

Biju reacted angrily, "Nana, if you offer food to the deity taking rice from that untouchable Harijan, would He accept it ? You take bath twice just at the sight of Ramu. Don't be clever. If you touch that rice, I will cut you into two halves."

A scythe in Biju's hand dazzled in the light of the lightning. Hari Nana fumbled and said, "Hey, I was saying so for the good of all. If the deity becomes kind, then this condition will change tomorrow !"

"Better stop. Henceforward take your deity to your home. Hey, Ramu, tell your wife to feed her child. That child is crying so much."

The towel was too short to cover the woman's body. Sanatana shouted, "Hey Biju, Banu try to find the head master. He does not belong to our village. Only for the sake of his job he came with his family from such a long distance, and stayed with us. Who else would take care of him other than us ? Moreover, he belongs to my uncle's place."

Satura said on his own, "We have never denied that.

I myself had gone to the school-building. The headmaster had told me that the scholarship money of my younger brother, Goura had arrived. Today I had gone there to fetch the papers.... the school roof was not there .... the flood had taken it away. Where do I find the headmaster ? I unfastened his cows, calves and ran back for fear of my life. Uncle ! my father and mother were drowned in the last flood and escaped from this trouble. I am troubled only for Goura."

That nerve-numbing, heart-rending night again danced before Sanatan's eyes : His father and mother are getting drowned... and his innocent child Kuna is jumping into the water and helplessly trying to save them. Sundarmani is shouting. He is too dumb to open up his lips. Oh, what suffering... How long shall he have to live keeping in his mind the memory of that sight ? He has nothing else to do. Satura's parents were drowned. He had not even a patch of land of his own. Satura became a daily labourer so that his brother could take admission in the M.E. school after he completed the primary education. What was that scholarship money ? Sahadeva told him only about the special allowance of the Government for the Harijan students.

Ratani cried loudly. She was – a distant relation – an aunt by courtesy. On some occasions she would think of her husband, and her daughter Kamini who eloped with a bus-conductor as she could not bear starvation. She shouted at everybody, and would cool down herself. Who she had after all except herself to console her ?

As such, they were Harijans. They earned their livelihood sweeping the yards of other people's houses. Her daughter used to loaf around. Only once she had gone by bus to her uncle's home. Ratani always narrated her tale thus : As she had no money, she would not go herself;

instead, she sent her daughter to her nephew's marriage ceremony. The conductor had told her that he would drop her daughter at the right place. After two days her daughter returned home, and she argued with Ratani and wanted to go away saying that the conductor would arrange a suitable job for her. She did not pay any heed to Ratani's words. At last, one day she went away. And there was no sign of her since that day. That very conductor still goes by the bus that comes to the bus-stop of the village. If he is asked, he says that he knows nothing of it. Kamini went to her uncle's house. What was his fault anyway ?

Six months ago, Biju had gone to Puri with his father and mother. He saw Kamini begging on the main road with wounds all over her body. Biju's mother dragged her into the bus, and surrendered her to Ratani. The neighbours looked down upon her. They ostracized Ratani, and did not give her any work. At last, Ratani took and kept her in thatched hut under the old banyan tree on the way to the lower ground of the village. The daughter was unable to recognize her mother; always she would be talking to herself like a mad woman. Ratani used to take a meal and sometimes some rice-flakes to her. She cried a lot, cursed the conductor, and the village deity. "Neither she nor her daughter is going to die"- she would tell Sanatana repeatedly and lamented. Once, even she placed the brass-ring of her finger at his feet, and asked him to get a little poison for her. Sanatana would stand speechless. What would he tell to such an unfortunate mother ? There is nothing more painful on earth than the pain of giving birth!

Banu shouted, "So many people are sitting here helplessly. The flood is advancing more and more. Whether we shall be alive tomorrow or not nobody knows. Who is going to bring here your mad girl ? Why did not you go yourself ? As if we have no other responsibility ? Grandma, please keep quiet, otherwise, I say, it would be no good."

The volume of Ratani's loud crying turned low.

Rangi nani said in a faltering voice from the other side, "Better stop. Banu. If food is burnt, it never tastes good. Let her cry. If she speaks something bad, it would really be a curse."

"Rangi nani ! you justify your name. Always you speak from both the sides. Haven't you yourself left your in-laws place ? You are really an ideal woman of our village."

"You, food of the Death ! I do not eat from your hands. Who are you to advise me ? How should I have stayed in my husband's place ? The moment I went there, I found that the rascal had already a woman at home. Not only that, but there were also children by him. My father gave me in marriage only out of greed for money.... but I could not stay even for two days there due to my co-wife's torture.... Haven't you heard this from your mother ? True, I came back. But I did not destroy the good name of the village like Kamini. I would be relieved if this flood gulped me.

All became quiet. What was there in Rangi's speech no one knew. Like chilly wind it froze their heart, in a moment. Again, Sanatana enquired about Sukadeva. He called his name twice or thrice loudly. There was no response.

Satura came near him and said, "Uncle, my mind is guilty of ominous thought. See, how the water is reaching up to the roof. I had closed the door downstairs. As the clay-supported door could not stand the pressure of water it collapsed. The stairs leading down are flooded with water. See how the clouds thunder in the sky. Even if we want, it is difficult to search for the headmaster in this night. Ramu knows how to swim... But what shall I tell him ? where shall he go ?

"No ! no ! Satura, no one should go out anywhere. We are even less than 20% of the village here. If anyone of us here is drowned, it will be a tragedy for me. Let the morning come, I shall move first. All of you now go to sleep. I am keeping a watch over the flood."

Hari nana loves food. He said haltingly, "Well, it is not necessary to keep watch. There is no place to sit, who can sleep here ? I have not taken a grain of rice since yesterday. Only I had some rice-flakes at night. How do I sleep, my dear ?"

None of them had anything with them. They ran away to save their lives. Ramu's wife had the sense of getting something for her son. Hari nana had cast his eyes on that.

Chakradhara is as old as Sanatana's father. He would be more than eighty. He leant against the railings in the roof. He suddenly laughed at Hari nana's comment. It is strange that man can even laugh being in such danger.

Biju said in a loud voice, "What? Why are you laughing, grandpa ? After grandpa passed away you eat once in three days, but you too ate thirty times a day. I have seen that."

"Hey, that is why all my young, employed sons could not afford me to keep half a day at their homes. Two of them are earning a lot. They can afford food for four to five outsiders. Only they could not afford to give food to their old father. Man proposes, God disposes. I felt disgusted and changed my eating habits, yet Yama (the god of death) is not willing to take me. Otherwise, should I sit here with this flood around me?"

Somehow Chakradhara's voice seemed mournful. He was struggling with life at the age of eighty. To divert the matter Sanatana said, "Uncle, come forward a little. Don't lean against the railing. The house is very old, the railings have become weak. Grandfather of my father had built this house; repair is not done even once. It may collapse at any moment."

Chakradhara laughed again and said, "My son, you should rather be careful; so, sit away from me. Don't worry about me. Your speech is as valuable as a lakh of rupees for me. May God transfer all my years to you. You shall lit my funeral pyre after my death, my son."

"Uncle!!"

There was a flash of lightning across the roof top. Sanatana saw that human beings were loaded on one another. One who was asleep, against his entire body others rested their heads. It was such a long and wide roof. About two hundred people could sit here for a feast during a marriage or any other ceremony.

If on that fateful day, his parents had come up to the roof instead of going outside, today they would have encouraged him like Chakradhar uncle. O' Leave it ! No use of thinking that ?

Would the roof collapse ? If it did, what could he do ? For him living meant seeing scenes of destruction ! He can't do anything else. Even it was difficult for him to know where the headmaster went. Would Kamini be there in that thatched hut ? The poor mad girl ! She would not understand the meaning of a flood or a drought. Rangi nani was now silent, so also Hari nana, only Ramu's son was wailing. Perhaps he felt cold.

Sanatana could not control himself anymore and asked, "Hey Ramu ! Why is the child crying so much ? you have got something to eat. Why don't you give it to him ?"

"Giving it, master. I have also given him a little rain water. But the child is down with fever. For two days he had fever. Where shall I get medicine now ? He is trembling in cold. I have covered him with my vest. But that one is also very very wet."

Sanatana's shirt was also completely wet. He had already given his towel. He took off his shirt and squeezing it threw it at him and said, "Take and cover him even if it is wet. Tell his mother to hold him tightly."

"She is holding him, Master !"

Still the child was crying bitterly, and one could hear guttural sounds coming from his throat.

Sanatana looked at the sky. Today is Sankranti (a specific solar day in Hindu calendar). It is raining continuously. Sometimes more, sometimes less. It is always like this during bad times. He felt hopeless. It is a long period since he heard that there would be a stone-dam. Even if flood came, river water would not touch the village border. So many elections have been held, so many panchayat members, chairman and M.L.As have come and exhausted them with their speeches. All said the same thing- they would build a stone dam; there would be no fear of flood or drought. Everyday he read about it in the newspapers. But each time, the same old story is repeated. Suka headmaster was right. Yes, he was. Once the stone-dam is built, there would be no more political tricks left in this village. The era of Gandhi has ended. All are busy making profits out of politics. Service to the country now occurs only in a dream. We are passing through hard times.

He felt lonely. If the headmaster took shelter somewhere, it is fine, otherwise his whole family must have been destroyed in the flood.

He called aloud, "Hey, Biju, Banu, Satura, are you all asleep ? Has Aparti come here ? He was the first to give us the news. I do not hear his voice."

Banu said, "Uncle, how can we sleep ? You know

Aparti. He is the real scoundrel. He must have fallen asleep, while keeping watch over the dam. Then those people must have dropped that medicine to break the dam. He is always intoxicated with ganja..."

"Oh, I am not asking about his intoxication. Where is he?"

"At first, he declared the news in a loud voice in the village, and then went to fetch his family. It may be that he has gone to his in-laws' place crossing the canal. Who is going to search for anyone now ?"

Sanatana did not answer. What was there to answer ? Did he not know ? Because an overwhelming loneliness was descending on people, and they felt anxious, he was just asking all these questions repeatedly.

Night grew. The night of death does not end easily. He felt very tired. Tried to close his eyes. Again, he opened his eyes. Anyway, Ramu's son was asleep. His crying was no longer heard. Some people were talking in a low voice. What would happen in the morning tomorrow ? Would these people survive without food, surrounded by the flood ? The bags of paddy, rice, lentils and rice-flakes must have been submerged in water or swept away. No one knew. The staircase was covered with water. There was no way to go down and check. If the steps of the old staircase have collapsed, then everything is lost ! Let it go, let everything get drowned. Let this earth filled with people be swept away in this night of death. After all, who has done anything being alive all these years ?

"Master, Master....... what is happening to my son ? What shall I do ? Please come...."

Ramu, who usually kept himself a hundred yards away and addressed him reverently covering his mouth with a towel, shook his arm and called him wailing. Do the village folk think that Sanatana would repair everything. ?

He went silently with Ramu, and touched his son with his hand. His body was as cold as ice. He was trembling and coughed like an asthma patient. He was not responding to any call. Eyes were closed. It seemed he was suffering a lot. Hari Nana came, and holding the child chanted some mantras into his ears. Rangi nani, Chakradhara uncle, all came and sat around the child. All were alarmed. Would the child pass away leaving them all behind ?

Chakradhara said, "I know. When a flood comes, two or four lives must go with it. The river is such a witch that it casts its eyes on the newly born babies instead of the old ones like me !" Hari Nana sprinkled on him some water in the name of God and just lay him down. "We have nothing else to do. He can save or he can take him away. It rained continuously for seven days in Gopapura, yet it was He who saved the people!"

The child's breathing slowed down. Sanatana returned to his own place. The night was about to end, the morning star was about to rise. The sky was cloudy. It was drizzling. The flood-water was flowing all around with hissing sounds. It seemed that the building shook.

Sanatana set down and put his face between his knees. He was going to sleep. He leaned against the railings. He had only one piece of cloth on his body, not another to cover his face. Yet his eyelids became heavy. And he fell into a deep sleep.

After some time, he got up hearing a peculiar sound. He opened his eyes and could not know where he was... His whole body trembled. A crowd of naked and weeping children, men and women cluttered on the roof of his house. What had happened? Did the flood reach the roof? While trying to get up Sanatana fell down. Perhaps Ramu's son passed away. Ramu's wife was running half-naked towards the railings to jump into the water. Biju and Banu held Ramu who was wailing too. Harinana, holding that untouchable boy in his lap was weeping. Even Rangi nani was beating her head and cursed the fate of man. Only Chakradhara was asleep right there. There was no cloud, sun rays fell on the roof.

Just at that moment the voice of the head mater was heard "Save me ... save me ... who is there ... I am being drowned..."

As if our God Himself on pipal leaf was floating away in the flood, and was shouting for help, "Save me, Save me." The headmaster held the branch of a big banyan tree and was floating away in the flood. So many cows, buffaloes, goats and human beings gulping water were also floating away along with him. They had lost the power to open their mouths.

Chakradhar uncle shouted, "Really a great danger is about to occur. That banyan tree is seven-generations old. It is now uprooted completely by this deadly flood. The head master was wise in finding a shelter in it. But he is now in such a great distance".......

Satura said " I leave Goura to your care. Let me go and drag that tree. It is not good that one who had come to our village to serve, die in front of us.'

Saying this, Satura jumped into the water. While others were thinking whether to stop him or not Satura swam through the water and dragged that tree. But it was a sky-high tall tree. It was very big; its branches were so large that it encompassed the whole lower ground of the village with its shadow. Again, so many ghosts and witches lived in this tree. They lighted up fire at night and would warm themselves. All kinds of birds chattered there. There lived cobras, male and female, of all kinds inside the four or five holes in the tree. Alas ! that old tree fell down. The headmaster probably took shelter on it with his family. Satura's strength was too inadequate to drag away such a tree from the flood. Satura was saying something, but it could not be heard. On the one side of a branch of the tree was the headmaster, on the other, Satura. Both were floating away holding on to the branch. Goura was wailing. Lest he should run away like Kuna, Sanatana held him tightly. But instead of coming towards the roof they were moving away in the opposite direction. Water was flowing over the tree. They were going down floating up, and down again. After some time, everything became quiet. Sunrays spread over the flood.

Chakradhar sighed and embracing Goura said, "Why are you crying ? Your brother must have found a shelter somewhere. That tree is seven-generations old. It cannot be drowned so easily. This flood will not last forever. Will not the flow recede?"

At that moment, a helicopter flew over their heads. Food packets fell noisily into the water. Not a single packet fell on the roof. The children cried loudly. Men and women shouted, but no one dared to collect those packets from the flood.

Ramu sat with his dead son in his lap. His wife slept near him tired with weeping. But no one had the courage to tell him to throw the child into the water.

The day grew. The heat of the sun was unbearable. The body felt scorched and so was the stomach with hunger. The children cried continuously. The women were almost half naked. The men were covered with towels or torn clothes. Their faces were shrunk. There was no sign of any helicopter, or any boat. There was water all around, everywhere the flood ruled. Strong young men like Biju, Banu and Kandura had turned pale. Goura was only twelve or thirteen year old. He became exhausted crying and with thirst and hunger, and fell asleep. There were flies all over his face. In spite of the scorching heat the boy was asleep.

Evening fell. The children drenched the towels in the flow, squeezed, and drank the water. Sanatana felt thirsty. Chakradhara uncle licked his lips sitting and looking towards the western sky vaguely.

Sanatana was startled when he looked at Hari nana. What was this ? This man sat there since last night staring at Ramu's son. Now he dozed and fell on the child. Ramu's wife sat there clasping her fore head. The body of the child was covered with Sanatana's shirt.

Sanatana called, "Ramu, get your son from your lap. There are no funeral rules in emergencies. Here we will..."

Hearing it Ramu's wife cried inconsolably. Ramu collected himself, made his heart a stone, lifted his dead son and slowly drowned him in the flood. Something happened to all those who were there in the roof. All of them including the little children started crying.

After many many days Sanatana also felt like crying. It was exactly like that day the pain he felt in his heart when Kuna was drowned following his parents. If he had followed them too on that day ! No, who would then have seen this scene ...?

Evening passed amidst weeping, and it was night. The speed of the flow of water had come down a little, but not its length. No one could say how many days they would have to spend there like that. Who would die first and who the next, it was not easy to know. He had such a great desire to convert this house into a school, and put his desire on pen and paper Sukadeva Sir knew this well. If he died now, then his own relatives would create problems. There would be so many troubles.

"Satu ! Satu.... !"

Who was calling ? It was Uncle. Poor old man, he could not walk straight. His sons worked far away. They made a room for him with asbestos-roof removing the thatched one. During summer, he would sleep on the ground floor of Sanatana's house. He never said anything to anyone. He would laugh if someone asked him anything. How could he expose the children of his own blood before others, and ridicule them.

Sanatana tried to find Chakradhara in that darkness and touching his legs with his hands asked "Uncle, are you worried ? you must be hungry. It must be painful for you."

"Not like that. Ratani gave me a little water drenching the end of her saree. I have drunk to the full. What I thought was .... if a flood entered the town, my sons would be in trouble. My younger son's house is situated at lower ground... he has two little children... their mother always does not remain at home. I am really worried."

Sanatana smiled even being in such a misery at the moment. The ties of the world are really strange. Man worries about protecting his family-tree until his death.

Chakradhara said again, haltingly, "You must have rice and lentil in your house. If I don't eat something tomorrow, I will not survive."

"It was there ... But whether it is swept away in the flood or is spoilt how can I say ? The doors and windows have broken down. Relief-party may arrive in the morning. All is God's will."

Chakradhara uncle breathed a deep sigh. People sat here and there quietly as they were totally exhausted.

In between the children cried out of hunger, and would become silent again after some time.

The night grew.

Sanatana felt very thirsty amidst that silence. Hunger moved like a knife in his stomach. He felt as if he had not eaten for years. Last night it rained heavily, and he had drunk a lot of water. It rained again in the noon and at that time also he had drunk a palmful. But now it was not raining, and he was feeling thirsty... What would he do ? Near the railings he bent down and tried to get some water. His hands did not reach the water level. He had neither his shirt nor his towel. The cloth he wore was drenched with water, sweat, dust and mud. Should he call Banu, Biju, Ratani or Rangi nani ? Rather it would be better if he took off his cloth, wetted it with the floodwater, got some water and finished with the job.

Who knows whether all were asleep or not ? Women cannot sleep easily. They must think about their children, near and dear ones. And looking at the sky they would be shedding tears for them. Mosquitoes, insects, heat and a suffocating atmosphere-all mixed up made it difficult for anyone to sleep. There was darkness all around, patches of cloud were there in the sky and a few stars twinkled. It was not very late in the night. But thirst and hunger obey no time, it attacks you in odd hours like a ghost.

Sanatana looked around the roof and tried to recognise the faces. Nothing could be seen. There was no sign of any movement. He could hear the sound of water only. All day he had seen the scenes of cows and buffaloes getting drowned along with the floating dead bodies of dogs, the dead swollen bodies of young man and women, old men and women. It was difficult to know who belonged to his own village and who were from other villages. Sometimes the floodwater would drive them away and sometimes it would push them up and down. It was disgusting to witness all these. Better one be dead. How could he, he thought, drink that water knowingly ?

Sanatan pressed his lips and tried to sleep. Few moments passed; wind blew a little, he opened his mouth and looked at the sky; and again, closed his eyes. Oh God ! If he could control his thirst till the morning, he would drink a palmful of water by pushing aside the floating dirt on water. It was difficult to see anything now in the darkness.

In the evening Banu, Biju and Kanduri got a bamboo pole that was lying there in a corner of the roof for ages, made a hole in it, pushed it down the other side of the roof, collected a little water through it and drank. That bamboo pole was however old and broken. So, the water that came through it turned half of its quantity when it reached near their mouth. He felt like laughing when he saw the scene of their exhaustion in drinking water in this manner. They would pull at a husk thinking it to be a coconut, pull the green plants thinking that it could have some fruits, pull the empty polythene bags expecting some relief-roti and boiled potatoes in them.... there was nothing ... two and half days already passed in heat, rain and cold. There was so sign of anyone. Neither the Govt. nor the non-govt. relief parties. Could not anyone come here ? It seemed the helicopter did not inform anyone after its return from this place yesterday. It dropped all the food packets into the water. It did not care who got the packet and who did not. But it flew twice or thrice over the whole village and near about places. Could it not know where happened to the people here, what such a tall banyan tree was uprooted ?

Time passed. Are there no birds anywhere ? The night tells time like a clock to them. Sanatana felt thirsty, yet waited for the morning. But that was not to be. Towards the last part of the night Chakradhara uncle haltingly said, "wa...ter."

"Uncle ! Uncle!"

Uncle was merely moving his lips. There was no sound anymore.

Sanatana was frightened. Quickly he removed half of the cloth he wore and hung it down into the water. When he tried to pull the end of the cloth, he felt dragged towards it. It seemed someone pulled and clutched the end of his cloth from below the water. When he tried to pull it again, he was dragged downwards again.

Before the cloth was pulled away and he became completely naked, he shouted, "Hey Biju, Banu, Kanduri... come... come... someone was pulling at my cloth. Clutching a stretch of the cloth, his dhoti tightly, Sanatan leaned against the railing of the roof.

Biju and Banu ran towards him. Kanduri followed. The children also got up. His behind was without any cloth. What could he do ?

Biju said, "Uncle, wait. Just be there. Your cloth is stuck in a thorny bush... Slowly I will bring it up."

Biju, Banu and Kanduri lifted up a thorny bush stabbing it with the bamboo pole. Nothing was visible in the darkness. Again, the pole was old and weak. Uncle's cloth had to be drawn up.

Suddenly Banu shouted, "Biju, Kanduri... see some-one is there in that bush. I think it is a woman. The cloth is entangled in her hair and is stuck in that thorny bush. She must be someone from our village."

Biju said, "Look, look, there are so many relief packets in that bush. Lift it slowly... slowly. Get that piece of cloth which Rangi nani is using as her pillow. We will lift up the bush with the cloth like catching a fish. Uncle, go to a corner. We will get your cloth, be sure of that."

Helplessly, Sanatana sat naked in a corner of the roof. He was trembling. He put his head between his knees. Hearing of the relief-packets men, women and children all gathered there one by one.

Ratani suddenly shouted ! Oh God!... perhaps it is my daughter Kani... Let us first see if my daughter is alive... she does not have a piece of cloth on her ... so what ... may she be alive. Hey, Banu, first get her from the thorns, then you will collect the food-packets. I know, it is my daughter, my queen, my rising moon. She has arrived here searching for me. I have not slept the whole night. My daughter was there in a thatched hut. That huge banyan tree was uprooted and swept away yesterday. But my daughter has come to me sheltering herself on that thorny bush. Hey, get those packets one by one... No one has any right on them. My daughter has brought them for me.... only for me. But shall I eat alone ? I am not at all like that."

Sanatana raised his head. Before they got Kamini out of the thorny bush, they all fell head and foot on the food packets. Kamini was lying on her belly. Her body was swollen and had turned into a log of wood. It seemed someone had torn all the packets and thrown the food into the water. Ratani was busy in caressing her daughter like a mad woman. All looked at it silently. There was not a single syllable sound. No one had the strength to lift such a big grown up girl and place her straightly and properly there. While he was going to pull his cloth, Ratani said, my son ! don't feel bad because she pulled your cloth... you give half of it to her, and bring my daughter to my lap... let me hold her lovingly to the end of my heart's desire."

Sanatana put half of the torn cloth round his loins, and lifted Kamini's head to Ratani's lap. Biju and Banu made her straight.

But what was that ? Kamini clutched a food-packet in her teeth. Her frozen hands also tightly grasped two more food-packets. Within seconds people started snatching the packets from her mouth and hands. The packets were torn but that could not be snatched away. All of them dashed against each other and fell over Kamini's body. She looked horrible, and such an unpleasant smell come out of her body that the whole atmosphere of the roof seemed poisoned by it. As soon as Ratani put her hand on Kamini's forehead, a layer of skin came out of it. People still fought madly for the packets in her hands.

Ratani was shouting holding her daughter closely against her belly. Someone snatched away forcibly the packet that stuck in Kamini's mouth. Pieces of wet roti scattered from that half-torn packet. The adult and the young, all fell over these. The flesh on Kamini's legs, hands and face virtually turned into a paste in that stampede. Who was going to listen to Ratani's wailing ?

Hari nana rushed forward and snatched Kamini's body away from Ratani's lap. He put his hands into Kamini's mouth and took out a piece of something. He shook it before all saying that it was a piece of roti turned black, and shouted, "I warn you all ! this is mine....... I have found it ...... I shall eat it." The children moved round him and cried. Sanatana became dumb at what he saw : While he thought that Hari nana might be playing a joke, and therefore while he felt light about it, at once Hari nana gulped that black thing. It was Kani's tongue or a roti, no one knew.

Some children were licking his palm holding his right hand. Ratani also became speechless at this sight. While

Kamini was moved to Ratani's lap, Chakradhara uncle breathed his last. What to speak of a pyre, Sanatana even forgot to give him a drop of water. It was good that he had not seen this; or did he die after he saw this sight ?

At this moment, Hari nana shouted, "Leave my finger.... oh ! I am dying...." A five or six year old boy chewed one of Hari nana's fingers as if it was cucumber. The finger bled profusely.... Still that boy was not in a mood to leave it. Kanduri slapped that boy and dragged him away, but that finger just hangs at its root.... Oh ! misfortune, Oh ! misery. Hari nana was crying out of pain. All looked at him with disbelief.

Ratani was talking to herself like a mad woman, "Let them all die. As they all burnt the life of my daughter, let their lives be burnt and destroyed. During the day they would say that the girl became a prostitute eloping with an outsider. They ostracized me. And I had to keep her isolated in a thatched hut. But they would all go there at night. They would not pay her a single paise. It is they who made her mad. I know everything. That old banyan tree was a witness to it all. The earth could not hear it.... could not tolerate it.... drowned them all. It was only my daughter who came back to me. Did anybody of any other people return ?"

No one could answer her. Even Hari nana was quiet inspite of the pain in his finger. Sitting quietly the children stared at Kamini....

Kamini's mouth was open. As it were, her lips parted listening to her mother's call. But her tongue could not be seen inside her mouth.

Sanatana was compelled to make the situation easy. As if he was born to hear and to see everything. Would a heart-rending morning like this ever again appear in his life?

He told in a loud voice, "Chakradhara uncle and Kamini left us. It is of no use thinking about them. Banu, Biju, Kanduri, lift them and drown them in the flood. Yesterday, uncle said I would lit his funeral pyre; but alas ! it is not in my destiny to do so !"

After drowning Chakradhara uncle when they were lifting Kamini from Ratani's lap, Hari nana said. "Wait my boys, wait a while. I could not light Kani's pyre, but I would drop a little of my blood into her mouth. It was only due to me she was socially isolated; lived near that desolate burning-ground in that thatched hut. I said that the deity would become impure due to her... I threatened not to offer puja.... but it was she who used to take care of me, massage my tired body with oil, used to wait for me... She never asked for anything... I too did not give her anything. At last, I ate her tongue out of hunger. In her last moment I would drop a little of my blood into her mouth. I have nothing else to give."

Drops of blood from Hari nana's finger fell into Kamini's mouth. Ratani pulled his hand, tore a piece from the end of her saree, tied it round his finger and said, "Go, now you are free from sin. It is not that you attained salvation, but you saved the village.... Now you can go.... go..."

All looked at the sight stunned !!!

Patadei

Nobody could know where did Patadei go leaving the home in the middle of the night. It was a full moon night of the time of the *Dola* festival. The moon spread over the entire locality in its white brightness. The deities were moved door to door to be offered the sacred food and were again placed in the fair-field amidst the instrumental extravaganza of *mridangam* and *jhanja*. The small children were again moving in the village-end after sleeping for a while. Picking handfuls of coloured powder people smear each other with it stealthily, as they could. The merry-making of 'Holi-day' can't be the same like that of the previous day. The festival comes once in a year, one can't catch it forever if one wants to. It comes and goes away with the blink of an eye. But even if you do not want to catch it, it comes pouring itself on you. The dust and dirt of the whole year lies over one's body and mind. Nobody can see it and it can't also be shown to anybody. And perhaps exactly so Patadei was laughing outwardly though, she had many worries within which possessed her like ghosts for years. In one such moonlit night, while there were festivities all around Patadei came out of home, having offered the sacred food to the deities, to see the fair. She had eaten a bowl of rice in water and fried leaves of drumstick tree in the evening. She rolled herself on a mat on the verandah near the kitchen as she had stomach-ache. Her father had gone to a far-off village bearing on his shoulder the statues of the deities. There was no one at home with whom she would talk a little. Mani bhauja from the neighbourhood had called her to play cards. But she refused to go saying she was ill, and laid there. Mani bhauja and others were back. While closing the back door, somebody said laughingly, "Eh ! she has swollen her body and slept like a wooden log and yet complained of ill health. For no reason..." Then all of them roared in laughter. Their laughter blew over in some unknown direction in the waves of the wild wind. But Patadei laid flat on back and gazed at the moon. The sounds of the crowd and merry-making outside did not touch her though it reached her. On that day she was there in another world and was thinking of something, it was not necessary for anybody to take care of this except herself.

The whole locality was overflown with devotional songs and 'sankirtan.' The people were smeared with coloured powder and were rejoicing. At that time of midnight Patadei locked the door and went out to see the fair with no fear for the nocturnal animals, witches or the ghosts. Nobody in the whole night bothered to open the locked door and to see where Patadei had disappeared.

There were celebrations throughout the night. In the afternoon all took rest in their own house after the colour-play was over in the morning and noon. Nobody had time to go somewhere and to see anybody's whereabouts. Moreover, there was a 'pala' competition between the two localities at night. Who was going to bother for Patadei ! After spending that night, when Jagu Behera- wearied and tired returned home in the next day noon hour, he saw the locked door and got annoyed. He called Patadei in a loud voice. But his own voice returned and dashed against his own chest. After sitting for a while he got up and went to every house to search for Pata while scolding her like anything.

Why shouldn't he scold? He had given Pata to marriage only after selling his five acres of land. The son-in- law was handsome like a prince. They had more than two acres of land including the plot of the house and had lots of mortgaged gold. But his daughter did not stay over there even for two months. She only knew what had happened to her. Within a month she became pale in worries. If asked, she never said anything and she only gazed blankly. As if she was seeing a human being for the first time or in fact, she was trying to more out something. Jagu thought that since he had brought up his daughter in a delicate way, she was facing trouble in adjusting herself in the new surroundings. She had no mother or brother to make her speak out the worries. Being only a father what more he could do ? He was not a rich man so that he would charge her in-laws with harsh words. But amidst all the works he was always worried for Pata.

Before anything was heard or known, one day at night the padlock of the door resounded clankingly. It was raining drizzle. The black cloud had flung upon the sky with its limbs wide open. The frogs were croaking in the pond-whole. Jagu was sleeping being covered from head to toe as it was cold. He woke up at the knocking sound. He asked twice-who was there ! Nobody replied. Thinking that it was a ghost-call he changed his side and again fell asleep. After some time again the padlock jingled. Jagu felt irritated, holding the sacred cloth of the Deity he opened the door and got shocked in the darkness. Whatever it may be blood is thicker than water. It was not at all difficult for him to recognize his own daughter in the darkness. Yet with speechless wonder he heard himself saying feebly- "Pata ! Pata you...."

Pata entered the home without saying anything while sidelining his father at the door step and bolted the hook of the door. Jagu asked worriedly-

"Hey ! How did you come in the middle of the night ? Did you quarrel with my son in law ? Did you come here secretly ?"

Pata stood with her face downwards leaning against the wall. Her face was not visible clearly. Shocked Jagu Behera managed to sit somehow on the floor when Pata moved inside the home without speaking anything Jagu asked in a painful voice-

Hey Pata ! what happened to you ! You are not speaking a word. Did your in laws harass you ? All are well or not ?"

Pata went inside without giving him the reply. Jagu thought that perhaps the situation had become little bit complicated. It will be known soon. Why disturb her at this odd hour ? Whether she had eaten something or not that also he did not know. She was always stubborn. He could not convince himself and got up to ask his daughter who was sitting on the kitchen yard. "Do you want to eat something, my child ? You may get some watered rice in the earthen cooking pot." Pata put her face between her knees and cried aloud. She wept like anything. She had not wept so bitterly when she had left home for her in-laws. Jagu wiped out the tears of her daughter's eyes in his own towel and kept quiet. Jagu understood that for some reason his daughter could not bear the suffering and so she had walked out. The reason will come out on its own.

Now she is inexperienced, later she would get herself adjusted to the situation. Next morning either his son-in-law or his father would definitely come. Jagu Behera would not leave them without warning. But that never happened.

Month after month already one year was gone, but nobody from Pata's in-laws come to take her back. Jagu tried a lot, but he could not find out the reason for which Pata had walked out of her in-laws in the middle of the night. If asked, she only gazed blankly. Her eyes got drowned in unfathomable tears, her lips trembled, but she could not speak a word. Jagu kept quiet to the queries made by the people of the neighbourhood. If somebody insisted, then Jagu would say his son-in-law had gone to Madras. After he got a job over there, he would come here to take Pata with him. But there was not even a letter from the mother-in-law or father-in-law or the son-in-law and nobody had come with a news. For some reason or other Jagu Behera also did not go to her in-laws to enquire about it. Whatever he got from his daily wage at this old age, both of them managed to live with it even though they had to starve frequently. Pata had never spoken on her own that she had become a burden for her father at the old age. What is the use of getting angry ? Even if he gets angry, he would not express it before Pata. Lest she might commit suicide or runaway somewhere ! He had no other one in the world. Whatever she may be, bad or good-disciplined or in-disciplined, he had to live with her ... he had to bear all fame or shame only for her sake. That is why a talkative fellow like Jagu became a tongue-tied one. After Pata came over here neighbouring people started accusing her. Someone told that Pata was driven out of the house because of her quarrel with the in-laws, another told that the son in-law had sent her away because she could not become of his choice. Some even told that Pata was beaten with burning rod and thrown out at night because she flirted with the neighbouring boys. Without saying anything to anyone Jagu looked at Pata. He thought that he would ask about it, he would admonish or he would forcibly take her to her in-laws. But he would stop doing anything when he looked at her tearful sad face. Soon after the dawn break Jagu went out for daily wage that would end in the evening only and then he thought to do something to solve this problem. He would not live forever to take care of her daughter.

Jagu could not control himself anymore. His body got exhausted after two days of tiredness and fasting. His daughter should have waited at the door step with food and water for him. Instead, like a newlywed bride she was playing cards or gossiping in the neighbourhood. How much Jagu Behera could tolerate ? As if he would be toiling and toiling only till he would be taken to the grave yard as corpse and he would be considering others sentiment. Would anyone ever come forward to take care of him ?

Jagu Behera shouted loudly – Pata ! Hey Pata ! where are you ? Come soon ... Pata ! There was no response anywhere. Jagu Behera moved from door to door in the whole village and when he returned home in the dusk hour, he found that the door was locked yet. As if the two broken doors were clenched with each other and were teasing him. After sunset darkness over his thatch spread all around...

Jagu Behera sat on the home yard leaning against the wall and dozed. He dozed off the whole night there and at dawn break he woke up with the sound of the crow and coucal. He looked up the padlock and the door was still locked....

The villagers and the onlookers said, Jagu Behera did not regain his sense from that dozed state. If the elderly people came to console him, he would look at them in blank eyes. If any girl or young married woman of the neighbourhood offered him *torani* his lips would tremble, tears would start flowing from his eyes, but not a single word would come out. They all whispered among themselves that the father got paralysed and became deaf dumb because his daughter became unchaste and broke her marital home. In fact, lying in that dazed state for ten days in hunger and thirst Jagu Behera slept forever. Next morning though the people of neighbourhood called him aloud he did not respond. But his two still eyes remained fixed on the padlock of the locked door. Flies were swarming up his face.

Three years were already passed since Patadei left home and Jagu Behera left the world. Since then, three fairs had been already celebrated in the grove-yard, seasonal mango flower buds had bloomed thrice and were prematurely fallen, the waves of the river were faced towards the ocean dashing against both of its shores. Mani bhauja became widow after having a son. Many of her friends were displaced through marriage. But nobody saw Patadei returning home. Nobody thought why Patadei left home, or nobody bothered where her husband had gone or got married to someone else. But like every other day there was sunrise and the seasons had performed their cyclical play. Patadei remained like an unspoken, uncared, unwanted question mark in everybody's mind. She was incapable of answering for herself   and no one else Since that day the door of Jagu Behera's house was locked like that. The house had only one and half rooms. There were only torn cloth, mat and a tin-box left inside it. All the people of neighbourhood had seen those things. Nobody had greed for that, why should anyone touch those things of the ill-fated, ill reputed ones. Everybody was afraid of ghost or spirit at night. Unfortunately, Jagu Behera's house was situated at the end point of the village. Since then, flowers ceased to bloom in the tarata plant that was there in front of the court yard and so nobody felt attracted to go over there for plucking flowers and in that pretext checked Pata's belongings by opening the door. Isolated and deserted, the house wore a view of a haunted dwelling. While crossing the road over there in the thin darkness of the evening people could see the physical form of Patadei clad in a white... Sometimes they could hear the piercing screams of Jagu Behera.

Suddenly one day there spread an uproar all around. The three years seemed like three decades. Things of the past was not recollected properly. Those who did not know anything, they added many cooked up fictions to the fact. Those who knew, they expressed their alarmed shock. The reason was, one morning Patadei was found brooming her court yard. A two year old boy was following her putting his two fingers into his mouth. Patadei had put on little fat on her waist. Her face and belly also appeared fleshy. But however, as usually before her eyes were expressive of pain and tears. The news spread all over within a second. Patadei, the outcaste daughter of Jagu Behera had returned home. She had also got a son with her. That must be her own, otherwise why should she have brought with her? The one who had walked out of home at midnight leaving her prince-charming husband, did she walk out for nothing? She could not stay at her maternal place. She managed to elope with someone again. Who would feed her and cloth her for whole life ! Since youth was passing on, she had no strength to live on her toil. At least she had returned to her maternal village with a hope for living.

There was hell and heaven difference between Patadei of yester years and that of today. Yet she did not care anybody. If elderly respected people questioned her then she covered her head with her cloth and stood with downward face. Sitting on the torn mat Patadei looked at the girls and married women who passed by her house in pensive eyes. She did not respond at all to the jokes and teases made to her. Sometimes she was smiling or sometimes drawing picture on the ground in an absent mind.

They all said that she was an unchaste woman. Let her live on her own. Who would bother for her ? Nobody had yet heard the story of becoming a proud mother after leaving the husband. In-spite of this she had so much of pride and vanity ! For heaven's sake God would never forgive her ! Was Patadei a heavenly deity so that she could do and undo things ? How she dreams of living on earth by fictionalising all the facts ? Shame ! shame !! . As if she could not find a little poison. How could she live in this world simply shutting up her mouth for everything ? Her lower primary education would not offer her any right direction in this regard. She had no father or brother to fall back upon. At-least one day the villagers decided that Patadei should leave the village if at all she wanted to save her life. Otherwise, that house of Jagu Behera will be set on fire. Patadei lowered women's prestige in the village and shamed all.

That day in the early hour of the evening when the people of the neighbourhood gathered together in front the Patadei's house and asked her for explanation, she pressed the tattered end of the saree on her mouth and said- "Yes, I am the mother of this child. When my husband left me in the next day of marriage and went away to Calcutta, both my father in-law and mother-in-law locked me inside a room and kept me in starvation without caring me for fifteen days.... Then I ran out of home secretly in the middle of the night and came to my father. Seeing me my father also became perplexed. While staying with him all the time I had to bear with the rebukes and insults from others. I had to bear up so much of accusations. My father had to toil at the old age only for my sake. Yet the struggle to fill the belly was not over along with social humiliations.

Patadei cleared her throat and stretching the cover on her head continued.

"I had nothing to say, nothing to do also. I could not die to free my father from hard toil... but... this cruel world made me return here again with a child."

Someone elderly came forward tightening the towel around his waist. Patadei could not recognize the face for her head-cover. Putting hand on the waist he shouted in a horrified tone-

"What did you say ? Would you repeat again ? Did the earth give you a child ?Why did it send here instead of keeping it sometime where else ? So, the saying goes ... the guilty shows a stubborn face. Tell me, just tell me whose child is it?"

Patadei stretched the cloth over her head once more and trembling horribly sat down on the floor. Tears were flowing from her eyes silently, there was suffocating pressure of anguish, but it was not voiced. Suddenly someone kicked her on her waist. Mani's mother in law, she happened to be her aunt by distant relation. Pata wailed, the old woman shouted.

"Hey, silent devil ! What was there in your mouth that blocked your speech ? You had been posing a disciplined girl since childhood, but you just could not manage to stay a month over there in your in-law's place. You killed your father alive. And now you are telling that you are blessed with a child by the mother earth. Tell me the truth who is the father of this child ? Otherwise, I shall make you into two pieces with my kitchen chopper. Yes, I mean it. You must take me seriously. Did you get my point?

The old woman was trembling while keeping her feet on the neck of Pata. Men and women were surrounded all around and were looking as if some farcical play was going on.

Pata's neck was pressed more and more. Her breath was chocking. There was fire in her eyes. The earth would not fall apart for her sake, nor Lord Shiva or Goddess Parvati would step down from heavenly abode to save her. She would die if she wanted so and she would also live if she wants. Is that all ?

Suddenly God knows what happened, Pata stood up throwing aside the old woman's feet like a straight and well-built woman of five feet height. A violet colour was exploded over her face with the mixed reaction of confidence and hatred. She gazed at the gathering of entire village with staring eyes, took the weeping child to her arms and said-

"Are you asking about the father of this child ? Look, they all are father of this child who are standing over there. Ramu, Beera, Gopi, Maguni, Naria and few more of them ! How can I name the father of the child ? It was full-moon night of Dola festival, there was pala competition on the fair ground then, and at that time it is this Ramu who gagged my mouth with his towel and lifted me on his back. They all jumped over my body and squeezed out my flesh into pieces in the bush near the grave yard. My mouth was gagged, but before losing my sense I could recognize their faces in the moonlight.... But whose child is it ? How can I say ? It is this Harijan Haria who took money from them and left me at Cuttack. I did not come here before so long because I did not want to share this with my father anymore. After coming over here also I did not tell anything to anyone... Aunty, now you ask them. Let one among them declare himself the father of this child.

Suddenly the situation became tense. The old and aged looked at each other. The young ones smiled jokingly. There came nothing exactly a question or even an answer from anybody. Aunty was sitting on the verandha as if tired and exhausted. Ramu, Beera, Gopi, Maguni etc. lowered their face.

Patadei started brooming the yard again while wiping her eyes. The little child started crying non-stop. Patadei kept the broom stick there, cleaned the flowing nose of the child with the fingertips of her left hand, took him to her arms, caressed him fondly and then said- "Why are you crying? My dear, are you afraid at the sight of these men folk ? Do not be afraid. My dear, am I not there with you ? Where is a male in the world who would identify himself as your father ? Do not cry for that, for you have a mother..."

What the child understood from that was not known, but clouds disappeared within. He leaped forward extending his hands towards the moon and he roared into gentle laughter. And as if the people gathered over there were shocked with that laughter, looked back awkwardly and started walking with lowered face.

A few flowers that were in blossom just two days back in the leafless tarata tree were smiling in the wind. Mani's mother in law was walking silently in half-bent waist while knocking down with her walking stick.

Patadei looked here and there spat in her son's chest. My God ! such a princely looking child became pale within a moment and this low people made him so by casting evil glance. Who is supporting her or who else would ever support her ? She is the rightful mistress of her parental home; she is the Queen- Mother and her son is her Prince.

At that time, the earth and the sky were not moving like any other day and remained motionless. Patadei was looking up and down and was laughing and crying at the same time.

The Interval

What was the necessity for her to go away so dramatically ?

If she had slightly hinted her problem, one would have saved oneself from needless explanations to many. She had never raised her voice against anything during her stay all these days. There was no sign of displeasure even in her gesture. Of-course nobody has time to notice such things even on a pretext.

What a strange thing ! Anita's mother is not at-all ready to take it as normal. She is not a small girl. Married on her own choice, she was never seen showing lack of interest in anything till she becomes a mother of three children. Of course, since her childhood she was a girl of quiet and detached temperament. But that did not mean that she would go away without any reason leaving her whole world. Definitely the usual conjugal friction must be the reason. Casting a look on her son-in-law Anita's mother clipped her lips and went inside the house weeping bitterly.

Digambar Babu put aside the newspaper and said-"Abhaya.........!"

Wiping tears from her face, Indumati broke down. She said in a trembling voice –

"You go and look after him ! Neither physically nor mentally I am prepared to look after this son-in-law."

"See, Indu ! I simply do not understand how Abhaya is

responsible for this. As one single mistake begets several others, you are opening up ways for each mistake in a clouded state of mind. There is no point in accusing Abhaya for nothing...."

Digambar Babu went to the drawing room. Nobody was there. Abhay's figure with his dishevelled hair disappeared through the front door.

Digambar babu tried to remember carefully. What would possibly be the reason ? She was so vivacious and lively, so clever and intelligent, and above all she was so calm and quiet, yet she would do such an indecent thing, he could not imagine.

This is the only scandal in his spotless life of sixty years. A married daughter running away from home like this specially when he is alive has put him in a state of unbearable shame.... fie on it ... fie... ! What would he say to anyone? Indumati would not understand anything. His own heart is neither prepared to accept anything nor to listen to any rumour. He searches for truth. Who would find it out for him? Where did she go ? Where is she now? It is very difficult to find her in such a big world. But is she alive? Is she...?

Digambar babu looked at the money plant that crept round the boundary wall. Last year Anita had come on the occasion of the delivery of her third child and spent a few days here. She has planted it with her own hand. But she is not here today – the plant has grown without care, and she had not bothered to take care of it even once. Why should she at all bother for the plant of which she is born ? But ? Somewhere there is a doubt. His heart is not convinced despite his efforts. How can he take it for granted that Anita had worldly sufferings simply because she had married on her own choice. Was she a saint or extraordinary ? What special quality Abhaya had to overwhelm for whole life an intelligent and good natured girl like Anita ? Marriage, family and children-are the only things in life ? or.... something else beyond all these .... what is that ?

Digambar babu looked at the road. His younger daughter Sarita, five years younger than Anita was coming with her full-fledged family. Now she would also ask the same question and Digambar babu would have to answer that ! Except him, no one was there for three days long in his house or in Abhaya's place to answer all these delicate questions. Sarita and Manindra stood on the steps-one on the higher step than the other. Sarita had the same question- not in her lips but in eyes. Digambar babu said mechanically-

No news yet, my dear. Where did the naughty girl run away ? Could not she even think of her children ?"

Manindra said-

"I had been there. But I could meet no one. The children were asleep and Abhaya babu was busy ransacking some papers and letters having bolted the room in the upstairs. I think we should have an eye on him now. If you and 'ma' could go and stay there ...."

"Don't worry Marindra ! No other accident would happen there. God is in heaven !"

Sarita said –"But where did apa go ? People all around are saying many things. Her friends, persons known to me and people familiar with Abhaya bhai have taken the incident to such a point that you can hardly imagine... !"

Frustrated in exhaustion, remorse and guilt for three long days Digambar babu shouted in an irritated voice- "Shut up ! I don't want to hear anything. As if I do not know what your friends, companions and well-wishers must have said and discussed. Should you explain that to me ? I want to hear what Abhaya is saying. What is his explanation for this incident ?"

"Bapa, why do you make him responsible for it for no reason ? An amiable man like him...."

"Ritu, I don't have to learn from you how to know people. Don't I know what sort of a boy Abhaya is ?"

"Yes, polite and perfect gentleman like him.... !" Manindra wanted to avoid the issue for a while.

Digambar babu said –

"Your mother has gone to sleep just now after weeping a lot. I don't think we should disturb her."

Suddenly tears came to the eyes of Digambar babu apparently for no reason.

Sarita and Manindra went back as they came silently.

Inspite of so much familiarity the dog barked after them.

Abhaya felt as if air and light stopped in his room. Papers, trunks, box, photographs, sarees, blouses – all lay scattered in the room. Nothing was found. She had not left even a small message as she went away.

As if the life of twenty three years meant nothing. Worthless like a handful of dust and stones. It is not twenty-three years. If you add the two years before marriage, it is really twenty-five years. Abhaya began to count the years by fingers. No, it is all right. He never failed in calculations .... yet .... ?

What did Anita lack ? She herself had wanted to marry him. Many times, before marriage she would whisper to me – "Tell me, you would be mine only ! tell me please ... tell me once that you are mine. All my dreams of life will be fulfilled if you become mine."

It happened so ! Without caring for the opposition of the world and against the wishes of their parents Abhaya had married Anita. He had given her all that she did not have in life. He had worked hard for the happiness ! But.... No ! Something pricks his conscience suddenly.

Anita did not know that. She did not know anything about it. She did not know his affairs with Sulakshyana. Neither Anita had gone there nor she had come here. No one had seen Abhaya in any embarrassing situation with Sulakshyana so that ... !

What would have happened if someone had seen him ? Who would have believed it ? If it was believed, how did it matter ? Is there any point in being tied to one woman simply because one was married to her ? The important thing is that he had not destroyed his bygone days because of his relationship with Sulakshyana like many of his friends who thoughtlessly torture their wives in similar situation. What does it mean ? One can have emotional satisfaction with a clever and intelligent woman. Having her support one can prosper in life. But the body needs a youthful fresh body. Sulakshyana was meant for his temporary sexual satisfaction. He had made a very calculative move and had never left a clue for anybody.

Then? Did Anita want something else beyond his reach? An ordinary woman – could walkout defying his name, fame, establishment-everything. What a pretension of love ! Abhaya become disgusted with himself.

He had never imagined that he would be fooled like this. Giving her so much of freedom was his mistake. Not only one or two-she has got hundreds of both male and female friends. Her time was spent on numerous meetings, cinema, theatre, intellectual discussion and argument. He never found Anita in a depressed or irritated mood. Who knows ? Perhaps a secret love affair .... What could be then? Who could be that fellow ?

Abhaya threw the glass against the wall ! The clattering sound resounded all around.

It is no other than that scoundrel Mohan ! Many times, Abhaya has seen there in the lonely drawing room talking to each other, listening radio, discussing politics. Sometimes he also joins them. Not only that she also talks to Suresh, Shasanka, Geetimaya, Pranabandhu, Uma, Savitri, Prafulla and Arun etc, goes to their places for dinner and also invites them. Abhaya joins them occasionally. And he has never heard a simple complaint from Anita during all these years. He could never imagine even in his whim that Anita can even spend night somewhere else. Then Anita ...?

Only one is possible out of the two possibilities. Either she has eloped with Mohan to a far-off place where no one would trace them out or she has left the world forever. No, no, she second one is never possible. She had a strange attachment with this worldly life. Her innumerable photographs at home speak it. Somewhere she is overwhelmed at the sight of a blooming sunflower in the garden. In other frames she dreams of a future holding her children on her lap, she beholds the sky resting her chin on the body of the car, emotionally charged with devotion her eyes a filled with tears as she prays in the puja room. She remembers the minute details of all the photographs both its time and place. Such a person cannot take leave of this world so soon. She does exist .... very much alive ... She has gone away to satisfy her unfulfilled sexual desires with a lover secretly. But who is that fellow ? Who has got so much of guts to destroy his happy married life of twenty-three years. Had he seen him, he would have crushed him into pieces- within a second. Coward !

Another glass dashed against the wall. Small pieces of dazzling glass were scattered throughout the room.

Nanda's foot steps are heard outside- a loyal old servant of this house. Abhaya opened the door slowly and looked.

"Babu ! the babus have come to meet you."

"Tell them that I am not at home. Yes, listen, does Mohan babu comes now ?"

"No, except him all others-same thing – asking about ma."

"Tell them no and remember, if Mohan babu comes, then ask him to sit in the drawing room and inform me"

"Yes babu, Mohan babu had come here in the evening just before ma left home .... He is not at all seen since four days. Should I go to his place ?"

"No, you just sit outside and get them all out. No one should disturb me. The children should not be interrupted."

Nanda left. Abhaya felt violent in anger looking at his way. Nanda also suspects Mohan ! He is such an old loyal man !

Like a mad elephant Abhay strolled throughout the house in furious excitement. This defeat of life and guilt feeling is only because of a woman ! How would he live his life with this ? The guilt is simply unbearable.

They were sitting around the table. It was raining outside unexpectedly at an odd hour. As if someone had tamed the wild swiftness of the wind with a caressing touch. There was an undercurrent of silent but unspoken sadness.

Uma threw down the magazine and said – "Whatever you say I shall never believe. Why should Anita at all go away silently leaving such a full-fledged family life. Simply I don't understand it. Perhaps she was hurt or humiliated...... She was too introvert to share it with anyone and she has left with that pain within .... she will be back .... she will come at right time....

While pouring tea from the kettle Savitri said rather irritatingly –"Why should we bring that issue here. Many such news is flashed up every day. So many people gone missed or dead, there is no limit to it. That does not mean that the rest would die for them !"

While smoking a cigar Shasanka said-

"No one would die, it is true. But what would happen to Abhaya ? …. How will he manage with three children without Anita ? This is too shocking to be a shock. You women folk, what do you know ? We also need social safety and security."

Dhira, Shasanka's wife was standing near the window looking at the sky. She gave a side glance at Shasanka and said-

"Man lives with body, but woman lives with heart. Once that heart is dead, no one can make it alive again. That heart of Anita had died since a long time. Why should she live. Many women in this world are feasted and fed, giving birth to children, living in luxurious apartments ... without any meaning... Now Anita has left, she has done no harm to anybody. To live or not to live or to do the act of living is altogether her personal choice."

Suddenly a silence fell upon the house with these words of Dhira. As if all of them were busy in smelling the smokes piped out continuously of Shasanka's mouth.

After some time, Suresh cleared his throat and said-

"We should not argue on these matters. Commenting on the internal affairs of another household or another's wife does not go with morals. The only justification here is that Anita and Abhaya both are our intimate friends. Anita's departure is like the sudden death of a dear friend...."

While collecting the tea cups Aruna said-

"Yes, as you say... The same question haunts everyone.

It is such a long familiarity. As if the day does not go well without meeting her once. At least if she had shared her feeling, we would have found a way out of it. We could have done something for her. However, if the final call comes, no one will stop it."

Aruna's last words made them more suspicious. Though all of them want to simplify and end the matter, somewhere lies a hard knot that no one can unfasten. They can see in their mind's eye Anita's pair of eyes that are enraptured with joy. So familiar and so expressive eyes... but everything went wrong.

Car-horn was heard outside Abhaya went out almost forcibly. Looking at his way Dhira said.

"Whatever you do, how much you search, you won't find her anymore. She is gone.... I asked my father through a planchette call, whomever did I ask, all of them answered the same...."

Uma said-

"Why didn't you call her then ? I don't like such second hand information !"

"I would have called her ... but its consequence might out be good.... She is gone just only and she might not be in a good mood. Besides, I love my family and children ! Leave it, what is the point of torturing her ?"

Dhira was becoming serious. She can't convince anybody with argument. She has no evidence to counter the belief.

Interrupting the silence Sasanka and Suresh entered the house. Mohan followed them as if leaning against an unknown shoulder. Mohan was not seen since the day Anita left.

Dhira got up worriedly and asked, "What happened ? Is Anita back ? Is Mohan babu not well ? Why don't you say?

"Oh, keep quiet please. Do not spoil the news with noises ? Can't you see Mohan's condition ?"

Dhira fell silent at Sasanka admonition. Really Mohan looked ill. His eyes red, and face a curious mixture of sadness and anger. It is not possible to predict anything.

Savitri silently offered a cup of tea to Mohan and asked in a mild voice-

"Mohan, do you know anything about Anita?"

Within a fraction of a second the cup-plate along with the hot tea splashing over Savitri's cloth fell into pieces and Mohan shouted- "Why do you all ask me ? I do not understand, simply I do not understand. Even Abhaya is accusing me of having a secret affair with her. Why ? Because I was talking to her. But what about Sasanka, Suresh and Arun ? Together we are friends. We have talked to each other, gone for walk, spent leisure together-yet we have not understood each other. Even after twenty three years of married life Abhaya does not understand her. And we ? None of us has touched the border of her world. Not even her parents. And returning after eight days now I am accused of such baseless allegation.... shame ! shame!"

Stunned, they asked in chorus- "Really ! you do not know !" Mohan forcefully shook his head in its reply- "No, no, I do not know, do not know at all. How can you compare a torrent of endless eternal time with an ordinary lustreless one like me ? I do not ever understand that.

Suresh held Mohan's hands and said- "Calm down please. They have wrongly accused you. Please, don't mind."

Tears came into Mohan's eyes.

"You see ! We don't understand each other, but we become proud of our friendship. I am not troubled by your words. It pains me for Anita. Just half an hour before I had seen her in the station...."

All asked at a time –

"Did you see ? Did you really see in your eyes ? Is it true?

As if coming to his sense Mohan said-

"Yes- I did see her – She was standing on the platform. I asked about her journey. She said, Abhaya is on an official tour to Bangalore. She and her children are accompanying him. She looked at her watch and went to the other side crossing the over bridge hurriedly. I did not see any impression of gloom on her face.... How could I know even ... And even if I knew, how would have I brought her back? Who am I to do so ? At least I am not foolish like you people!"

An explicable silence pervaded the house. No one dared questioning the other face to face. It was not necessary also. The darkness increased in many folds in neon-light far more in density than that of black fortnight. Each of them was too self-engrossed to be aware of other's presence....

A sub-plot to the plot itself.

Digambar babu was returning from morning walk holding the hands of Mitra, Anita's youngest daughter. Situation was coming back to normalcy after one month. But there was fire inside the ash, he knew it well.

"Jeje ! Won't ma ever come back again ?" Mitra asked helplessly. As it were Digambar babu was the only reliable man for all future predictions.

Startled, Digambar babu said, "yes, yes, she would obviously come back. Just she has gone for study..."

"It's lie, jeje, she has gone away. Right ? Jeje, ma has left bapa, is it true ?"

"Who said so? All this is wrong ! people are jealous of your mother and so they are talking all such nonsense."

"Well, jeje, is ma married again there ? Ritu mausi told me that she has got sons and daughters like us."

Digambar babu knows it well. Now Sarita is simply mad after her father's property. And so, she does not even hesitate to infuse such unknown fear into the mind of this innocent child.

"No, no, all lies Mitu ! Your mother would come back..."

"I know she would return. She was the wisest one among all in this world. That is why she left leaving all behind. Is it not better to live away like this than dying bit by bit every day ?

Mitu wept and said.

"No ! You write a letter to her that she should come back soon. If you write her that I am weeping here, she would come back. Otherwise, I won't eat...."

Controlling the tears in his eyes Digambar babu said – "yes, of course I shall write a letter to her like this – My dear Nita, come soon my dear. Whatever new message you have got, come with that. We feel suffocated in the old rotten news, repetitive voice and a rusty stereotyped world. We have become so poor, so lifeless, dull without you – Do come for once and see.... I shall write to her explaining everything."

"Jeje, do not cry. I won't ask you to write letter anymore.... Whatever you say, I shall obey...."

"No, my dear ! She would not come back unless I weep. You also cry. Everybody should cry- the trees and the creepers, the birds and the animals, everyone will cry – then only my Nita will be back. While leaving she shared anything with anybody. Only she had left a few lines on a small piece of paper – "Bapa, I am leaving. I do not know the place, not even the reason. But since few days everything is not going well with me... Lest I should get any meaning of life after going out of the four walls... then I will come back... I am not sure about it.... But I know that

I will come back. How can I tell you the nature and mode of appearance as I do not know it myself... That's all. This cruel world could not understand her, did not weep for her, did not recall her – how would she come back ? Mitu, you do cry. Cry more. Nita will return in varied forms, in many languages, many lives and souls. Then everything will change. Don't I know ? Don't I know my daughter ? I know her ! She will return. You just cry. I will also cry, everybody will cry, then only she would return spreading the essence of laughter... Nita .... would come... she would definitely come. She would talk about new things breaking all conventional beliefs... she would create new belief... You just cry .... cry, my dear....

Mitra, the eight years old girl was stunned hearing such deliriums of Digambara babu. She has neither seen so much of tears in the eyes of her grand pa' nor she has found him talking so much standing on the road. Digambara babu continued saying all the same things loudly in the middle of the road. So many passing vehicles and people were witnessing this scene gathering near the two sides of the road.

As if frightened helplessly, Mitra made herself free from Digambara babu and ran forward in the crowd.... As if the entire world was running after her like a robber to fall upon her.

Who knows what was the tide of time in the flow of life then !!

Father

When he paddled the bicycle towards home with a whistling sound it seemed his father was sitting on the verandah. As he was sitting earlier, exactly like that. He used to sit leaning against the left pillar and putting the two clenched palms on his two knees. Sometimes the head would lower a little. Sometimes he would sit putting the red towel on the head that was about to be bald. Sometimes he looked at him while entering with the bicycle and sometimes he could not. If he were too late, he would warn mother with few harsh words.

Usually just before the day of his death also he took horlicks from mother while sitting on the verandah. He settled the account of vegetable seller and fuel-wood-seller and went to bed after taking bread with milk. The only exception was that he did not get up from bed and watered the plants, nor did he knock at the door of Subas's bedroom to make him arise early. Hearing the wailing of his mother and younger sister Rina, Subas got up from bed and came to know that his father died while asleep. He had not said a word to anyone before his death. Within a minute a number of friends and relatives gathered over there. Before he could bear the initial shock Subas had to perform the funeral rites of his father and returned home. Subas had no time to think of his father because of the frequency of all these events. The house was so crowded with people that Subas never thought of whether the owner of the house was present or not. Gradually he felt lonely within as the crowd of the house started fading. He never thought that he would be so lonely like this in the absence of his father.

Subas's hands stopped on the handle of the bicycle. What was he looking at his father was sitting as usually... face downward. He rubbed his eyes out of fear and looked again. He stared at the verandah very carefully. No, it was not so-an illusion of mind-a ray of street light had fallen on the verandah through the foliage of mango and ring worm tree. As if the wind was playing hide and seek with light and shadow. The suppressed loneliness of such a long period had taken a weird shape and was standing before him. Subas looked around. The street wore a desolate look. No one's voice was heard at home. Rina must be sleeping with her head on the study table. His mother would be sitting in the prayer room offering puja. It is not possible to think specially in such lonely moments that the man who was watching the check-post of the house would never return again.

Subas got really frightened. He had no belief in ghost or spirit. But whom did he see on the verandah ? Just one month back he himself in his own hand lit the funeral pyre of his father. Then- ? He called his mother twice in a hazy voice and pressing his face on the bicycle he closed his eyes. An emotion-charged cry made him shivered from head to toe.

Perhaps his mother was awake or she could hear his cry or she was waiting for him near the window. She opened the door at Subas's call and running towards him she caressed his back and asked in an eager tone-"Did you fall down somewhere ? Why are you standing like this ?"

Subas tried to control himself and kept quiet. Looking at the tree, wall and hedge his mother said in a mixed tone of sadness and mild admonition- "How many times I have told you not to work so hard day and night. You have inherited this odd nature from your father ! you don't listen to anyone ! Stubbornness is the trait of your entire folk. Now come inside, it is too late !"

Subas told in a cold voice-"Suddenly my head started reeling. So, I called you. Are you not frightened ?"

"Get frightened ? Why should I ? I was waiting for your call. I do not know what has happened, I am not at-all feeling sleepy."

His mother avoided his question. In one way it is good. Subas, twenty three years old young man would get frightened like a small boy at the sight of his father's spirit- why should she think at all ?

Stepping up the verandah he took a side glance of the pillar. There is nothing. The same hide and seek play of light and shadow is going on. The entire verandah is quiet and still.

Keeping the bicycle inside the house Subas looked his father's photograph hanging on the wall. When he pulled the chair and was about to sit, his mother said-

"Why are you sitting again? Wash your hands and come, I would serve you dinner. Don't you know the time ? You were so carefree because your father was there !" His mother's tone was little indistinct and it was left half said.

Carefree ! He was disgusted hearing his father's short lecture on his dark future. He was making him conscious by saying ten thousand times a day that he had become penniless after giving four daughters in marriage. That means he wanted to say that he had left nothing as such for Subas so that he would roam round with a bicycle from morning to evening on the plea of searching for job and would exhaust meals only. Yet his father did not know that even after his death Subas was going on like that though he had changed a little. Because in spite of his hard effort a chance had not come yet so that he would change and be someone. He also did not know when it would come.

Subas took a loaf of bread and soon after he put a little curry into his mouth his face became pale. Now a days his mother was not in a good mood. She was not aware of what she was doing and what she was saying. Most of the time she would sit and gaze blankly. More than that the servant boy had gone home after two days of his father's death and had not returned yet. Should not Rina do little of household work ? All his anger hurled on Rina. He called her loudly- "Rina, Hey Rina ! Are you only eating and sleeping ? You know that there is no one at home – how will mother manage all the works ? Every day there used to be a sweet dish for dinner or there used to be meat or egg... Now everything has stopped. No, I cannot eat like this."

While Subas was about to get up, his mother forced him to sit by holding his hand and said- "Don't be insensible. What would Rina do ? Your father is no more...."

His mother wanted to refresh his forgotten memories. Even when his father was alive, he was not earning raw cash except his meagre salary. Whatever paddy they used to get from the village, they were selling it and managing with it. Subas had never thought that mother would remind him of his father's absence like this so suddenly.

No one's father lives forever in this world. As such his father had no good relationship with Subas. If they sit together, there would be only argument and misunderstanding. For a long one year their relationship was limited within only 'yes' and 'no.' He supervised the farming land without taking loan even in a clerical job, he had given four daughters in marriage and had left a two-room house to rent for his future security and comfort. By saying this repeatedly he wanted to exercise his authority over Subas. But he had not accepted that. Subas felt revolting because his father had termed his duty as his ability. He felt as if his father's two shrunken eyes were following him.... criticising all his activities in its minute detail and was saying satirically that Subas is a worthless fellow, he is of no use and that is why he goes on loitering the whole day.

He also used to go out in the evening, would return home late night to find that father was sitting on the verandah leaning against the pillar, and had not his dinner yet. How much late he made to return, he would find the same one scene. Without asking anything mother would serve food on two plates by arranging seats side by side. Looking at the dinner plate father would say... "Hey Basu's mother, why did you give me so much of dessert ? Take it and give in the other plate." Some other time he would say-

"Give little of sugar to Basu, cream his bread otherwise he won't be able to eat. After all he is your darling son !"

Mother would do that work mechanically. But what was there in his father's tone God knows, Subas would get irritated the moment he heard it. He was not a small child anymore that his father would tell him such things.

He could not do anything in life, but does it mean ...? Many times, Subas had thought to give him a straight cut answer. But he could not do so. He thought of giving such an answer after getting a job or if an emergency situation would come. Before that chance comes his father left for ever. Like any other father he did not call Subas to his death bed and holding his hand did not say few words nor even he shed a drop of tear. He had neither love for Subas nor confidence in him. And again, dramatically his mother asked him to eat quietly because his father is no more.

Subas threw his mother's hands in disgust and got up. He bolted the door and laid down in bed. He felt like revolting against everyone. His mother in her pale face wanted to make him conscious that his father is no more and that is why he would have to control his anger and giving up all comforts and pleasure he would have to manage himself with self-restraint and without thinking of bad or good of anything he would have to accept everything ! While his father was alive, she was telling this in a silent expression and she was not ready to listen to anyone except his father.

Now she is vocal and is repeating that line - "father is no more".... so what ? Does it mean that nobody would go on one's own will at home ? Will he sacrifice his likes, dislikes and everything for ever ?

Subas got up and stood near the window. The dim street light was falling on the wild flower plants planted by his father. Every morning, he would hunch over the plants weeding out grass. And bending down he would water the plants with a joy. Again, after bath he would come and pluck flowers for "puja" while murmuring a mantra. Today morning only, he heard his mother telling somebody that knee deep of grass has grown there because father is no more. The wind spread over the leaves producing a whirling sound.

As if Subas got startled and sat on the cot. He felt burning pain of hunger in empty stomach. He was not feeling well because of this unnecessary irritation. Did mother and Rina have dinner ? Who is going to enquire about all that ! He has no time to take care of himself. Since eight or ten days he has been moving from 10 O'clock morning to 6 O'clock evening and yet he did not get a job anywhere.

After his father left those relatives who were sympathetic enough to arrange a job for him, now they are behaving as if they do not even know him. He is unable to meet them even after waiting hours together at their home. Subas does not have faith in anyone. Exactly like his father his friends are all indifferent and unfaithful. He has also no one as such... Why so ? Why ? It is only because of his father. Since the day he could sense he had been hearing his father's orders only. Sit here, don't go there, read this book, so on and so forth. He had strict instruction for him not to make friends and thereby not to create problems at home and outside. Even he was telling ten times a day that if he did not pass with a first division then his future would be totally dark. In spite of so many irritations it was strange that Subas had passed in first division. He had almost no friends at all and obeying the rules and regulation he was also returning early in the evening. If by chance for once or twice he got late his father would stare at him without saying anything. That was more than enough. Sometimes he would sleep without food after having argument with father on politics and would try to maintain gravity by not speaking to anyone. But father was like that only. Even though he had a bad habit of exercising authority throughout his life, but he was getting worried if he found any disorder in Subas's eating and sleeping habits. His worries were surfaced while scolding mother without any reason, finding fault in her cooking and getting Subas's clothes washed by Rina etc. Subas had never seen him lowering his head before anyone. He justified that fact and also accepted death quickly.

A silent dissatisfaction was suppressed inside Subas. His mother was knocking at the door. Subas simply did not understand the reason of making him so irritate. He was surprised when he opened the door. Holding a bowl of hot dessert his mother was waiting at the door. When he caught her eyes, his mother lowered her face and said- "The curry did not taste good and so you ate nothing. Take! Have a little of dessert!" There were tears in her eyes! What nonsense! Who told her to make such farce in the middle of the night? He felt like throwing the plate of dessert.

"Have a little of it. It is too late now. If your father were there..."

"Take out, I won't have it. If father were there, would you have a rainfall of gold ? I do not like to listen that anymore from you people."

His mother looked at his face in wonder. As if she was looking at an unknown person. Subas could not bear that innocent look of his mother at all. She has not become a destitute because father is no more.

"Now it is your home. It will run according to your will. It will not run only if you get angry. You remained carefree because your father was there. Now my dear, you cannot go on like that. You have to take responsibility of the household." His mother said the same thing again. Subas was breaking into pieces in anger. No, he had no sympathy for his mother! She got scope to tell so many things because his father is no more. Once again, his mother told in a tearful tone- "Keep that front door closed before you go to sleep. Anything can happen at any time. And that too you get scared of such things. You are afraid of the shadow. If your father were...."

Subas threw the bowl of desert and thundered.... "How many times would you tell me that my father is no more? While he was alive what else more he meant to me and now... had I... I been an orphan?

While collecting the scattered dessert silently his

mother said gravely, "why are getting angry? Anger only suits to capable man. You would never go to sleep without food like this if your father were there. I shall do according to my ability only. How am I managing myself and home...... God only knows that."

This time Subas's two legs trembled terribly. He knew that his mother had the usual complaints against him. These are only expressed in his father's absence. All at home and outside want him to be "father." They want to see him as and in 'father' (role). As if nobody is ready to bear with the fact that Subas has an existence of his own and Subas's personality is different from his father's. Why? Pressing his lips together Subas sat down on the chair. His whole body is burning in anger. All have warned him strictly not to speak harshly to his mother in this situation. He is not able to keep himself in control though trying a lot.

Without saying anything more his mother picked up the bowl and went silently. Rina would have gone to sleep since long. The servant boy is not at home. Did mother eat or not ? The front door bolted or kept opened ? Who will look after all this ? Since more than a month he has become tired of this responsibility. It is not easy any more to live like Subas.

With much hesitation he got up and went outside. The door was really left open ! The bicycle was kept on the verandah ! Shame !...... the bamboo gate of the entrance was also open ! He took the key from the drawing room and went to the bamboo gate. There are periwinkle plants on the left side. The leaves have turned pale without water. The place is filled with weeds. The leaves of the banana plant have dried.

Subas felt pain within. Now he would go and clean

everything. The moment he started going towards the tree as if someone said, "son, don't go near the tree at night."

Who ? Subas was startled. As if he heard his father's voice clearly. He closed his eyes in fear and when he opened it, he saw his mother standing there. What happened to him that nobody knows, Subas laughed excitedly and said, "Mother, you go to sleep. The house seems so lonely because of father's absence. I could not sleep. Let me cool my mind and then I shall go"

"Are you mad ? Will you move outside because your father is no more ? Come, come inside. Gradually everything will be alright. Just as people adjust to everything in the world. Your father has told me this several times. Can I sleep at home when you would be moving outside missing your father in his absence?" Telling this in a tearful tone his mother cleared her throat.

Subas got embarrassed. What does his mother really understand ? He said in a fearless tone to avoid it-

"Lie ! who told you that I am missing him ? When he was alive, we had never talked nicely even for once. Because he died- Mother ! you have understood nothing really." In the meantime, his mother had come closer and was looking at him in sorrowful eyes. Looking at his face in speechless wonder she said haltingly-"Basu, you have got dark circles under your eyes ! I have never got a full look of you since your father died. You are not eating properly... missing your father. Would he ever return? Basu ! see, your shrunken cheeks... why should I live and not die ?

Mother wiped her nose and eyes with the end of her saree. Subas could see his mother's bony face with cheeks shrunken. She has also deep dark circles under her eyes, bulging veins in hands. Her long and bare hand is fixed on Subas's shoulder like a stick. While trying to overcome his sadness Subas became conscious. It is nothing. Like his father it is a new way of her mother to keep him in her control. No, he won't get swept away. He has had enough of it. No one has ever consoled him for once even though he has been burning within to ashes. Where was his mother then ? He could not remember his mother ever speaking a word of defence in his support when he was getting scold from his father !

Turning back Subas locked the gate and holding his mother's hands moved towards home silently. He smiled at himself for his behaviour. If an analysis is made then the conclusion will be like this- his father is no more, so he is supposed to manage himself like father. The moment he thought this, his hands started sweating. The strong palm that was holding his mother's bony palm shivered terribly.

Hardly he stepped up the verandah mother said – "No, we won't go home now. Sit for a while on this verandah. You will feel better with the cool breeze." Basu sat immediately. He knew that mother has spread net all around him. She may catch him at any moment. Subas's heart was beating. Mother said slowly- "How will it do if you remain so upset ? Do things remain same forever ? This shall pass too. And nobody's parents live forever. I feel as if it has happened yesterday only.... after one year my marriage your grandfather passed away. I was cooking, your grandmother was drying paddy, your father had gone somewhere. The old man said that he is having chest-pain. Drinking a glass of water at a stretch he slept facing the wall and never got up again. Back, your father cried dashing his head, your grandmother resounded the locality and village in her wailing for the whole day. Yet he never returned. Your father roamed like a moving ghost without food and water." Subas got irritated and said-"Why do you make me remember the past ? Father was like that, I am not like him."

His mother smiled faintly and said – "I know you would say like that. All of you are from the same mould. Like you his cheeks were shrunk, there were dark circles under his eyes only for missing his father. He gave up food and water... became almost mad without being able to bear the shock. Today you look exactly like your father in those days. Your father was not highly educated. He had a lot of confidence in you."

Subas stopped and asked-"Do you want to say that I look exactly like him ?"

"Yes, you are like your father-stubborn, peculiar and somewhat idiosyncratic."

Subas said gravely-"I had a belief that you will understand me. But I feel sorry to find your sense of understanding is just like others."

At once his mother brought his head to her lap and said-"Leave it ! It is only Kunti who knows Bhima's strength. I have to tell all these things because your father is no more today.... otherwise after having dinner, you would have gone to sleep silently."

Subas put his face in his mother's lap and cried loudly. How helpless is he really ? How much pain would he bear at home and outside because his father is no more ? Oh, why did his father die ? Putting his face in mother's lap for the first time Subas was searching for his father's existence in the darkness. And he felt like saying forcibly-"Father ! where are you ? Come back. Come back father ! I want to live like Subas only. I want to be a stubborn, peculiar and idiosyncratic Subas. Father ! as you were in your childhood !" But he could not utter a word.

The Tongue of Fire

Somewhere she has seen that in a film-the heroine never forgets to write a few lines hurriedly for her near and dear ones at the last moment of her life, when she decides to take leave of this world. As she remembered it, the bulk of rice in Nirmala's palm dropped. But whom would she write ? she has no one so dear who would stop for a moment after reading her clumsy farewell letter, or would raise a hue and cry after hearing the news, and do something dramatic. She tried to remember but no sympathetic face appeared before her mind's eye. The bulk of rice dropped from her palm and every grain was scattered.

After finishing her meal when she stood up to wash her hands and mouth, her mother in law shouted at her – "Hey daughter in law ! why, after all, yourself quite educated, your parents may be illiterate and poor-that does not mean that they haven't taught you manners ? There may not be ever a pinch of salt at father's home, but look at the daughter's pomp ! She is throwing away bowls of rice... as if her father has registered five acres of land in her name... Don't think that you will sit here like a queen, simply because you are married to a golden boy like my son, if you do not get all the things from your father within a fortnight, then take poison and die. One's dignity is more important than anything else!"

Nirmala's hand dragged from her mouth. Her

whole body shook with a terrible feeling of shame and humiliation.... Her tolerance and patience have reached a breaking point after so much of harsh treatment and starvation for those six months. She is neither illiterate nor incapable. She has managed to pass the matriculation from her village school. She knows what is right and what is wrong. She is not an illiterate and a fool like her sister Bimla who took poison and committed suicide without any protest against her in laws. She looked at her mother-in- law's face and said, "What is my fault that you should accuse me like this? My father has given dowry as much as he can. If you had any grievances, why did you agree then?

Instead of washing her hands with water from the mug, her mother in law threw it down angrily on the floor. Beating her head with her hands she loudly called out, "Hey listen ! do you hear ? O Naba, oh my dear child, my only child, oh my dear Nabakishore ! where are you ? I can't bear anymore such beating, kicks from your educated wife.... I can't bear these anymore."

Nirmala's father-in-law appeared at once. Soon he was followed by Nabakishore, Nirmala's husband. Nabakishore's uncle who was taking rest on the verandah as it was a hot day also got up and ran towards his sister. Nirmala was as it were struck dumb as the spectator of such unheard of melodrama. Before she could say something her mother-in- law said crying,

"Oh, my dear Naba ! Is this my fate ? How can you bear it as my son ? It is for you I suffer like this ! Listen ! your father had arranged a girl with a B.A. degree along with ten thousand rupees for your marriage, but you agreed to marry this one from a beggar's home. I had to give my consent. She does not feed me, does not respect me and instead she is beating me throwing the mug of water at me. Hey, do you lack girls for marriage. If you say, now, today I shall arrange and present few brides. None of the neighbours would find fault in dowry or gift during festivals ! only considering your sentiment....

Her mother in law put the small bundle of cloth on her mouth and tried to calm her fit of crying. Looking at Nirmala in sharp eyes Nabakishore said.

"Did I know it, mother ? what to speak of wealth and prestige, I did not even want anything from anyone. When her bridegroom threatened to go away from her marriage pendal, if he was not given twenty thousand rupees, and in fact when he got up to go out, the villagers just lifted me up and sat me on marriage pendal.... what could have I done then ? That did not mean that they won't pay even ten thousand. How would I have known it ?"

Leaning on Shyam uncle's body and walking her mother–in–law said-" Hey Naba, I can't stay with such a wayward daughter-in-law! You decide-whether you want to see the dead body of your mother who gave birth to you, the dead body of your wife. It is for you to decide. If you do not bring ten thousand from your father in law, my prestige would roll on the streets in the village. And once the prestige goes, I won't live... I am not a daughter of any mean family. Even in those days my father registered five acres of land in your father's name, and preferred to become a beggar wandering village to village than to lose his prestige. This miserable woman would eat up all my wealth...why should I live at all ?"

After her mother-in-law entered her bed room, Nirmala poured water on the rice plate, and while she began to get up, beatings showered on her back all of a sudden. Holding her waist she collapsed on the floor. Nabakishore thrashed her black and blue and was scolding her in vulgar language. Even if she lost her life no one in this house would come and check. Nabakishore-she knew this for a long time having been battered a thousand times. But this time he is blood thirsty. Does anyone know this ? Unconsciously a cry for help came out of her mouth and wafted in the wind shaking the silence of night. Hearing it her father in law said-

"Stop my son, stop why do you make your hand dirty by killing a mouse ? Send her to her father's house tomorrow. Write to your father-in-law that he should bring his daughter back with ten thousand rupees. Otherwise, we know what to do. If he can't pay in cash immediately, he should mortgage five acres of land or else let him arrange in his own way."

These last few words of her father-in-law spread into Nirmala's mind while she was about to lose her consciousness. These words were painful, more heart rending for her than the pain of beatings. Nirmala had no way to know when she lost her consciousness.

Nirmala herself did not know since how long she had a dream sleeping on the verandah of the kitchen. Suddenly she got up from sleep and found that she had slept with her head on the dirty rice plate with water in it. Her body ached. Head reeled. She could not understand where she was. Slowly all the events crept into her mind. She decided to escape in the night from this home. The day she had stepped into this house she knew she would not survive here long. She had prepared poison for that reason and thrown that away many times.... She had decided to cut off all attractions while looking at the pond full of water, but thinking something she stepped back. She had refrained from setting her body aflame. That is why she had decided last evening that she will not commit suicide. She would go away from this house to the town, at least she has got the qualification to manage herself...while having her food she thought of scribbling something before leaving the house, all these terrible things happened so suddenly !

The bridegroom whom her father had arranged insisted on taking twenty thousand rupees before the ritual of tying the marriage knot. Who would come forward to marry a girl who is already engaged to marry someone else? Again, the priest was also not allowed to chant the mantra keeping the bride's hand on the hand of the bridge groom. The money had to be produced first. Otherwise, the bridegroom would go away from the marriage pendal. My God! The whole body shivered at the very thought of all this. One would hear her mother's wailing from the courtyard. Her father had become speechless.... what could he have said ?

He was father to five daughters beautiful like fairies. But they were girls after all ! He could not be overwhelmed with joys because they were not sons. Her father toiled hard on the five acres of land to maintain the family. The two elder sisters were married somehow and managed with difficulties. They had to go through many humiliations as their father was not sound financially. When their suffering became unbearable, they would come to their father's place for a day or two but again considering the difficulties of their parents they would return to their hell. Seeing the fears in their eyes, their physical pain and the dense darkness for their future, Nirmala was bewildered with fear in her lonely moments. Yet they stay in the house of their in laws.

They survived bearing beating and kicks, and holding their breath under all pressures. They have given birth to five or six children.... but her cousin Bimla's condition was the worst. She had to suffer so much torture as she had given birth five daughters one after another. No son. Alongwith starvation and beatings her husband's neglect and indifference was most painful to her. Her mother had nothing in her father's place. Where could she get a dowry for her ? At last, Nirmala's body trembled in fear. Why did the villagers make Nabakishore sit on the marriage pendal ? True, the original bridegroom went away, but a moon never appeared in the sky of Nirmala's fate. With repeated tortures from the day, she was married she had turned into a stone. In the half unconscious state on the marriage pendal she knew that the ritual of tying the marriage knot was over with someone else. She had become a bride and daughter in law mechanically.... As if all the dreams of happiness of a married life turned into ashes on that marriage pendal itself. Nirmala knew that she could neither give happiness to others nor she get it for herself. Being a matriculate, she could know that it was necessary to be the owner of immense wealth in order to get happiness in this world. Neither beauty nor virtue is anymore the means of happiness. Otherwise, would an engineer bridegroom leave the marriage pendal, and she married to a village tout and smoker of "ganja" like Nabakishore who had not passed even M.E. School examination and showed up himself living off his father's money-lending business ? Who has made this law that an engaged but rejected bride could be married to dumb cattle, stone, tiger or elephant-anybody. Else she would commit suicide because she had no right to stay in her father's place. The village folk would look down upon her. She would not be considered fit to stay in her in law's place in this birth either. But what is her crime ?

Nirmala stood up. Her head, her whole body trembled. No, she would not tolerate so much suffering. Like her sisters God had not given her the strength to bear this agony, nor she had energy in her body and mind to control her situation. Why should a person who has no past, no present, no future hope for a life of comfort ? life has no meaning in this world except going through suffering without one's fault. Had she not understood this that she would dream again ?

The moon in the sky was about to set. After some time, like every other day, the bitter and burdensome poisonous morning would break. But why ? What was Nirmala's crime? All lived happily, why not she ? Cousin Bimla died. No! The world did not stop for her for a moment. Her husband married again, and lived happily ! None of the neighbours, the village folk, the elderly people in the village-no one opened their mouth. What would these village lose if Nirmala ran away from house or hanged herself or got herself drowned in the river or pond ? Her father in law, mother in law, husband-waiting for that occasion.

It seems sparks of fire darted from her eyes in anger and anguish. Then all the girls would die in this manner in this village, in her father's village, and in any other villages ! All would show pity, but what would she and the other innocent ones like her get from this ?

No, that won't be so Nirmala looked around her. There was silence all over. She opened the back doors and went out. The whole village was quiet, would it continue forever like this ? the world would not change if she died. Instead of dying if she runs away, then too it would continue like this. No, she must not stop the progress of the earth. She would set fire on the face of the society and burn it to ashes. She would destroy the system of opportunist men.

Slowly Nirmala entered the house and closed the door. No, she would not run away from home, hang herself or drown herself in the river or pond. She would die, but she would not let anyone live in this village. She would burn all in the village, and destroy. She would let the world know her reactions. Yes, certainly yes, she would kill, and die. Like her sisters and cousin, she would not free herself alone, and keep quiet. The fire she would light that would spread its tongue and lick away the whole world, the opportunistic social system...

Nirmala entered the room, collected her torn clothes and tied these on a stick again. She poured out oil from a lantern on it, and lighted a match stick to that while opening the back doors. There was a lot of time yet for the sun to rise. Oh ! Nirmala got angry with herself. Why did not she write a few words about her and leave this at home ? Leave it, her future generation would certainly appear to read her unwritten autobiography. They would clean her body mind and the burning fire in her. They would certainly give shape to her story.... Yes, only they would quench her all-consuming fire. On that day she would be born again, yes, she would take birth, marry, become mother.... not only she.... all those who were dead, tortured like her-all of them would be born again. A new world will dawn on that day.

From somewhere an unknown bird's voice startled her. Nirmala ran out with the burning stick in her hand. She set fire to the thatched house of her mother-in-law and ran setting fire to one house after another. She set fire to all the thatched houses of the neighbourhood and ran wildly like a mad woman. She was shouting on her own. She was calling aloud. She was crying. She was laughing. Even though sparks of fire from that stick fell on her saree and it had caught fire, she did not care, and ran like a hysterical woman.... forward and forward ! At her back a storm of fire was created burning down houses, neighbourhood, all prestige and tradition. But Nirmala ran forward because in front of her lay an unending forest. She knew that once the forest caught fire there was no escape from it until everything was burnt down and destroyed. A naked Nirmala was running into the forest to demolish the imaginary border of that unending forest.... Tongue of fire darted in her eyes !!!

Chameli's Tea

"Hey Buli ! here comes my writer Sab! Get a little milk from the pail that is hanging inside the room quickly my daughter ! The water starts boiling !" The moment Chameli sees me, she would call loudly for milk and dust the broken bench with her torn and dirty saree's end. She wears an innocent smile on her face. Buli gets the milk hurriedly and salutes me. It is her mother's order. If I go there to have tea for ten times, then also Buli would touch my feet for ten times. I find it difficult to say for how many times I have to bless her !

Chameli's tea stall remains open till 12 or 12.30 at night. It also remains open till one or two hours after the second show cinema is over. It extends more in summer days. In winter Chameli covers the end part of her saree around her and smokes a pipe twice to let out the steam. She leaves the door half closed and lightening a lantern she goes on sitting in the desolate rainy night...! As if she is awaiting for the eternal age of time ! Sometimes Chameli dozes off there ! She just forgets to get up and to go inside till the next morning. If someone asked the reason of keeping the stall open till the late night hours and sitting there sleeplessly, she would smile and say – "I am not giving anything free to the customers. So, whether it is day or night there is no point in disappointing them." But I do not remember anyone queuing for tea in her stall after 12 O'clock at night.

Half an hour after the second show cinema when I come to the road to relax myself for few minutes, I get fascinated by a far off image of Chameli's tea stall and sitting there cosily. I go and sit there- as if someone drags me over there ! Then Chameli calls Buli in her opium-addicted tone........ then comes tea in a glass. This is my as usual routine work. I feel as if Chameli keeps waiting till 12.30 or 1 O'clock at night only to serve me tea. Better quality of milk, neatly cleaned tea-glass and better coloured tea all are meant for me.

After being transferred to Baripada, Samaresh left his rented house for me to stay. Introducing me to Chameli he said, "you know Chameli, he is a writer ! give him nice tea, he takes tea for many times." Chameli snatched the words from Samaresh's mouth and laughing in her toothless mouth she said-

"What did you say babu ! writer.... writing stories.... it is so good ! May you live long .... may you live long ! I have asked so many people...... Nobody listens to me ...... !"

I asked Samaresh, "What ! what Chameli is saying to all, and nobody listens to ?"

"What will you get ? The old woman talks about her life – asks to write it and get it published.... Now you find her like this, but when she talks of the old man then you will see her real picture. This is her habit. Once you start listening, you won't get rid of it." Samaresh told winking at me.

This is long past now. Every day I used to visit Chameli's tea stall eight to ten times a day. Perhaps I happen to be her first customer in the morning. After returning from the office if I cannot take tea sitting in the stall. I sip cup of tea leaning against the bicycle... For the sake of decency only we do not have any friendly get-together in Chameli's stall. We have to go to hotel for that. But I do not know my steps are dragged over there in lonely moments. There is enriched liveliness in the act of looking at the sky while sitting on that broken bench in the quiet hours of the night. I do not know... exactly do not know why my feet get dragged over there every day, especially in desolate night. After I leave Chameli covers the wooden board. As if she keeps on waiting only for me. When I would reach there being tired of walking – that is her only botheration and so she would be waiting every night.

It was a moon lit night. Month of March. Spring wind was blowing slowly. The second show cinema was already over since long. I had already exhausted ten pieces of Charminar (cigarette) while walking on the road. After walking a lot finally, I reached Chameli's shop. Chameli was sitting- her posture moulded like a serpentine insect ! Seeing me suddenly she got worried and said a little irritatingly – "More, more delay ! Now no milk to make tea ! That rotten rogue – the earthen pail should have hit his head ! He would have been injured and died... He has come to torture me only !

I understood that these hard-hitting words were directed against someone else. But suddenly who had come here for Chameli could not blow out his head striking it with the milk pail. After a pause I asked – "Who had come ? You were talking of striking with the pail! That too milk-pail !"

"Why are you asking that ? Who else would come ? The one- my bread earner – my vermillion and bangles had come ! Otherwise, who else would come to take care of me after long thirty years... Let he be burnt, let worms eat him away, let him die a wretched death like that... just I did not look at his face!"

Suddenly her talk sounded unclear. Chameli started

talking to herself. I said – If you won't say the name of the visitor just give me a cup of tea. Let me go. I am feeling sleepy!"

"Who else would come ? He has no contact with friends and relative. Done nothing for his family. Why should they care me as a daughter-in-law ! Who else would come ? It is Goli's father.... He has come at the old age to eat and sleep in a palace as if his parental property is kept here. If he comes again, what to speak of milk pail, I shall hit his eyes with burning coal fire and kill him. I don't have a little of sympathy or attachment for him.... I shall kill him giving blow after blow.... What does he think of myself ? It is me ... Chameli... yes !"

I felt like roaring in laughter. I came to know that Chameli's husband has returned after a long time. I had a doubt. What is the necessity of returning after such a long time ? And if he came, rather Chameli should be happy. After all he is her husband ! I could not help saying –

"Now that he has already come ! Where else would the husband go if not to wife ? After all he has married you on sacrament....

"You please go ! I warn you, do not come to my tea stall any more. What did you say- I had married on sacrament ? What sacrament ? At the time of marriage, I was only twelve or thirteen years old-how can I know sacrament or religion ? Goli's father was more than thirty years old then. What do I know then ? My mother has tied me only for money.... It is nothing else Babu ! It is nothing else !" Chameli's eyes filled with tears ! The sorrowful pain of old age for the lost youth overwhelmed her for a moment. Chameli started on her own-

"That I do not mind Babu ! But I can never forget the ill-treatment of that fellow. Many other girls also do marry aged husband and live happily. Do not just ask about Goli's father.... don't ask.... What torture this body has gone through ! I made myself stone.... hardened my body... Hardly a little watered rice was available even once in four days at such a young age. What to speak of cosmetics like oil or turmeric paste. He goes out in the morning and returns in the late afternoon or sometimes in the evening or even in midnight. There is no one all around. I was the only one in that desolate house. I feel frightened. Bolting the door from inside I keep on sitting in empty stomach. If someday I happen to get a handful of rice, I cook it and eat with a pinch of salt... otherwise nothing ! Like this Babu, so many days, nights, months and years passed ! Now if I think it, I get angry on myself. Had I walked out of home at that time I would have lived like a queen today. Destiny could not tolerate me; can anyone change one's fate ?" Perhaps Chameli took breath. Her cough choked throat sounded violently noisy. To let her know that I am listening to her mindfully. I cleared my throat and started smoking.

Suddenly she said – "It is too late now, better you go home. What will you get out of such talk ? If I start telling all, it will be an epic like Ramayana ! Chameli cleared her stuffy nose. I looked at the watch- it was about 2 O'clock. As if a sad tune of an unknown pain continued in the mind, eyes are burning. I won't be able to sleep if I go to bed also. Aparna is not at home. She and the two children have gone to Berhampur to attend the marriage ceremony of my brother-in-law. So, it does not matter if I spend the whole night here.

I said-"No, you tell me. Let me hear. It is not yet time. The show is still going on .... !" Telling a lie I stopped. She did not protest. Today she has forgotten the time in her own sorrow. To begin with I said "Hey Chameli ! Did your mother sell you.... !"

"Taking two hundred rupees she got me married overnight. I had no sense of judgment then. I would eat nicely and can have ornament and cloth. I sat on the altar with this hope... But just see my fate!

"Goli's father is an opium-addict. He smokes pipes, drinks alcohol, what to speak of betel and drugs. His eyes always look red like onion ! I was frightened at his sight, Babu ! You are a godly man – I won't tell you lie. One day I thought to run away- I would commit suicide either by taking poison or drowning myself in the river. But death even could not touch me. I was four months pregnant then. I thought of my child... just could not give him up."

"How old were you at the time of Goli's birth?" I asked.

"I gave birth to Goli at the age of fifteen only ! His father was not there at the time of his birth. He went to Rangoon (Kalimati) saying that he would find a job there. She left me with my mother and told that after making the arrangement of a house he would come and fetch her. Babu ! What to speak- it is so painful I just feel like crying. Mother used to feed herself by doing odd jobs. After few days, my mother also could not support me. She started ill-treating me. It is true that now I have forgotten everything. That poor fellow has left for heavenly abode ! We should not say such things to elders.... But how can I erase everything ?"

She took little breath. I felt that Goddess Laxmi is going to appear after churning up the ocean or a leaf-less tree has caught fire in an unknown dense forest. Holding her hand I said-"Chameli, do not keep anything secret from me ! I shall write a story on you ! I shall let the whole world listen to your story. Do not hide anything from me.... for my sake please tell ! Tell me everything, frankly."

Chameli smiled faintly and said –"Will you write a story on me ? Who will read that ? the smallpox- deity has already taken one eye of that rogue ! Instead of dying somewhere he has come here to torture me!"

I said-"See, you are disturbing the flow. Tell me what happened after that. What did your mother say ?"

"Exactly so ! Do I have memory now ? One day Nakhi a relative sister in law in the neighbourhood came and said –"Hey ! why are you not applying oil to your hair ?" My hairs have grown rough and dry without oil. I had not even a grain to eat. How can I have oil for the hair ? Nakhi dragged me forcibly to her house and brushed my hair with oil and dressed it. The moment I returned home in the late afternoon my mother burst out in anger. The language she used to scold me is never used by any mother to scold her daughter ! finally he pulled my bunch of hair and cut it with a scissor and said –"You silent devil, are you not ashamed of? Husband is sleeping with whores in Rangoon (Kalimati) and wife is dressing herself up and is dancing here ! Go and die, I would get rid of you ! I am earning for you by milling rice in this age. I gave you in marriage so that you will look after me. The wife who cannot possess her husband should not live at all ! Should she live to earn bad name by getting involved with people ? Are you not getting poison ? You are getting dressed ... !" So on and so forth that I do not remember now. I spent the whole night weeping. So many thoughts came to my mind. For what anymore ? Goli was one year old. His father forgot both of us. Whom shall I wait for ?"

"Next day I went to Nakhi and asked her to find a work for me. Her husband is the head of the coolies. He took me and got me engaged in the construction work of a school building two miles away from the village on twelve annas payment per day."

"Few days passed. My mother did not go for rice milling any more. With money the same mother changed again. One day he felt sorry and said-"My daughter, we are poor fellow, I cut your hair, did you feel unhappy? What more happiness is there for a woman who is deserted by her husband !"

"Babu, my suffering did not end with that. God knows where Golis father was and how he got the news – after two months again he came ...!"

Chameli paused! I was afraid of looking at her face. As if fire coming out her eyes. Few moments passed. Chameli laughed herself and said –"What shall I say, Babu ! One day when I returned from work, I found him sitting comfortably on a wooden seat at home ! I abused him in whatever way I found. That shameless male was laughing. Had he been a male with self-dignity, he would have left immediately for the abuses that I hurled upon him. You know what he did ! The neighbouring people gathered over there. He simply prostrated himself before me! The neighbouring people were taken aback ! I was afraid ! I will incur sin for that ! Isn't so ? The wife only suits at the feet of her husband...! I do not remember what he was telling then!"

Suddenly I felt like laughing for what she said- "Goli's father is exactly like any other male on earth. God himself stretched out on the ground and touched His wife's feet, what to speak of others... Of course it is difficult to say what situation one faces... !"

At once I became conscious. Chameli was weeping while telling her story- "What shall I do ! I have lived with people in the society Goli's father stayed. As usually he was taking ganja, smoked pipe, had wine betel. Gradually he started taking opium from mother. He was sitting at home and I was going out for work. I was feeling awkward ! What to tell about his drama! Until I return from work, he would finish cooking, cleaning house .... shame ! ..... shame.......... I feel so angry ! But I cannot say anything. At night he would come and massage my legs, press my forehead.... what to tell you.... you are like my son !" To make it light I said-

"Why did you feel shy ? All the males give massage to their wives, press their forehead. When women do these things, there is no objection at all !"

"What are you saying ! I am not against doing such things during illness. But Golis father started saluting me all the time ! I did not know that he had such ill intention ! He had layers of complex inside... Every day he would call me in a new name ! It is he only changed my name 'Nakhi' and called Chameli. From that day only Nakhi died, Chameli is alive Babu ! she is alive...!!"

Nakhi's sister in law caught jokes hearing such a name ! I said- "No it is Chameli." She laughed at me.

"You know, what did he do at last ! He played treachery. One morning I found that Goli's father is absconded. Without telling anything, without informing anybody he ran away ! The wooden box left broken. He ran away at night with my two earrings, two silver bangles and twenty rupees cash. The most shameful thing- he even pulled out the 'deity-blessed' gold that was tied round Goli's neck. How can God tolerate him ? Is he a father or an agent of death ? Let him die- let him go to hell !"

I said – "Why are you scolding him like this ? Whatever has happened...!"

"What did you say ? Shall I not abuse him ? Will God forgive him ever ? The male who cannot feed his family, an idle fellow unwilling to work- that is a different thing.... But looting my wealth he would dare bringing my co-wife ! Hm....! Then I wept a lot ! Making a knot at the end of my saree I promised that next whenever he comes, I would blow out his head ! By that time, I was pregnant for the second time. It was difficult for me to work.... ! That is also not granted by God ! The baby was born on the tenth day of Goli's father's absconding. But he was lucky – he was still born! Had he lived, he would have reached your age now...!"

I saw that Chameli is weeping, tears flowing down from her eyes ! It is beyond my capacity to console her. I waited. She began on her own-

"Babu, what else more after that ! My mother expired just after fifteen days of my son's death. I sent letters through many people and yet Goli's father did not come. The people in the neighbourhood tormented me like anything. One day at midnight I stepped out of home along with Goli. Any way I managed to get inside the house of Senapati Babu's house, you must be knowing that house on the square of next locality. Nothing was known to me.... The Mem Sahib was so nice ! Now she has left for her heavenly abode- She gave me shelter in her house. But her sons were not disciplined. The old man and his wife brought me here. They had a big cloth shop there- they made a wooden living arrangement for me there. I thought something in my mind and started a betel shop. My daughter was growing. I would have to get her married. It is not a son so that I would sit quietly keeping him at home. Days have been passing. With so less money I have to manage myself and think of daughter's marriage."

"But do you know Babu ! Sena Sab's wife is a Goddess. She arranged a bridegroom for Goli. You have seen my son-in-law. When I have gave marriage-farewell to my daughter I cried a lot. Both daughter and son in law called me to stay with them. I lived a hard life all these years. Why should I need comfort now ? Though they may not tell me anything straight, they may think it otherwise. I shall earn my own living. Let me manage like this till my body supports me. Yes....Yes, it is Samar babu who guided me to open a tea stall. He is a nice man. He brought all the equipment for me. Of course I repaid it within a month. It is past seven years now. All attachments were disconnected ... I was waiting for death. But again, this Buli is not leaving me. She is a child and I feel attached !"

Chameli stopped. I know that her talk has come to an end. The dawn hour begins in the sky. But she has not told the real point yet. So, I was forced to say, "You told that Goli's father had come ! "

"No, don't utter his name ! God knows who gave him the information. When I was boiling milk in the evening someone came and sat on the bench. His hair had tuned white- also the beard. His skin was shrunken. Perhaps he was drunk and so it was smelling bad. He has no shame at all. Seeing me he showed fake tears in his eyes and said- "Chameli dear, I spent the whole life searching for you everywhere. You are here. You don't even bother to inform me. How stone-hearted you are ! Why is he alive ? Once again, he has come to show his drama. I lost my temper. I said , will you go or not ? Else I shall smash your head. Hearing my words he laid down at my feet-I threw milk pail at his head. The pail got struck against the bench and fell into pieces-I do not know whether his head is left without injury. Since then, I had closed the door and opened just when you came.... How do I know ? Dead or alive ? Who will lit his funeral his pyre ? That jackal - that dog !!!"

I said- " Chameli ! how can I see Goli's father ?"

"Why should you see him ? He is a hard-core addict-won't be able to deal with gentlemen. Babu you may go now. When he knew that me-his bread earner is alive, will he leave me ? You will see him again loitering here like dog. This time either I will die or he will die. Shall I create scenes on the street of this town by keeping this old rag in my house ?"

I got up. Chameli was crying. Let her weep. I did not have words to console her. I moved towards my home. My body has become wet with dew. With a plan to sleep the whole Sunday I returned to my residence.

Soon I put my feet on the steps my younger brother handed a telegram over to me. I opened it in trembling hand and read – Aparna has informed, Chinu is seriously ill. He should go soon. Train time is after one hour. I was worried almost like mad for the sleepless night, exhausted body and moreover Chinu's illness.

I did not remember the time I went to the station and got into the train. The train was moving without stop... while thinking of Chinu's sick- pale face and Aparna's exhausted tearful eyes. I could also see Chameli's tear soaked and shrunken face.

Actually, Chinu was seriously ill. Aparna has been tired. Chinu has become week due to fever. He cannot be brought immediately. We will have to wait for at least eight or ten days. Those days were spent in worries... Finally, a date was fixed to return. Chinu was coming after complete recovery.

On our return trip I told Aparna about Chameli. Of course she heard mindfully. I told her to show Chameli's shop on the way to home. I was thinking, poor Chameli, what happened to her, God knows. Whether Goli's father returned or not... suppose he returned, would Chameli beat him with a broom stick really.... would Chameli be happy if dies ?

The train stopped. We picked up a rickshaw. My mind filled with delight while nearing Chameli's shop. Coming closer I pointed at the shop. But what is this ? Normally the shop is not kept closed at 4 O'clock I felt like calling Chameli, Chameli. I would change my dress after reaching home and come, I thought. Children got down from the rickshaw and went home. My younger brother came running towards me and delivering a paper he said "Brother, that tea stall owner has asked to give you this letter." For what I do not know-my heart trembled violently. I opened the letter –

Babu,

I am an illiterate; I have not learnt alphabets. I am dictating Goli. She is writing for me. You would search for me after you return. Hence, this letter.

I had told you everything about Goli's father. But Babu, man proposes and God disposes ! That day when I closed the door, till the next five days I had no meeting with him. On the sixth day itself two persons from the village came. I came to know that Goli's father had fled to the village straight from the shop that day. Hardly few steps are left to the village, there is a river. While crossing the bridge he stumbled over there and fell unconscious after vomiting blood. The village people returning from the market lifted him to the house. After two days he regained consciousness. He is lying unconscious in high fever. There is no one to give him a drop of water, barlee or sagu. Who is there? The neighbouring people are not at all coming to him. He has sent these people by giving them my address. Babu, what shall I do ? I just cannot bear. After all I am married to him. How can I eat and sleep comfortably while he is dying there ? The village quack is saying that it is leprosy ! Relatives and neighbours are not coming at all. It is unbearable for me that while I am alive, he would suffer so much. It is the call of blood ! Will he really be cured ? I sold the shop, the utensils and somehow or other I managed to arrange five hundred rupees to take with me. Rest is on God ! Babu, do not mind, if I have said anything odd. Do not write story on me. The one who would have read the story is sick. And what is the point in disclosing the privacy of the house before the outsiders ? I would be only laughed at ...!"

I could not read the letter anymore. I was blinded with the tears of my own eyes !

Aparna came running and said – "Hardly you have entered the house, and you are crying ! It is not good for the children. Come, come. You will be mad for writing so much !" Holding her hands I said, "Aparna ! just stand by me. Let me cry for a while... please stand quietly for five minutes .... for I need a shoulder to cry on !" I was crying-

The Shadow of Darkness

The drum goes on beating. Almost two hundred students are doing drill standing together. They are in blue frock and white ribbon. One-two-three dum dum.. dum...dum. It feels good to see. Even for a moment the busy eyes of unknown persons turn around.

With that beating sound Koili comes out of home holding the little naked child and covering a shabby cloth of her mother on her torn pant. She comes running towards the field but stands a distance. She hesitates to go close. She cannot stay for long also. The drum beats when she is cooking rice or collecting cow dung to make dried fuel. As if the magic flute of lord Krishna in Dwapara era is being played for her. In whatever condition she is, she comes out. But she never forgets to bring her younger sister in her arm. As if she thinks of something and stands at the side of a corner of the boundary wall. Someday she stands for a long time and some other day for a short time.

Every day holding the iron rod of the window I look at the young girls who are doing exercises. My eyes search for my daughter Rosy in that gathering. Whether she is able to perform drill correctly, how does she look while doing this it is very necessary for her body-fitness so on and so forth.... I become absent-minded with all these thoughts. When my eyes fall on Koili.... what she is thinking of ...what she is doing. It is really strange. Sometimes after the drill is over, she performs drill on her own displaying her limbs like that. Standing in the deserted field she becomes conscious and fears lest somebody might see her. Poor fellow-yesterday as if the accident occurred right in front of my eyes.

Perhaps Koili was doing drill standing in the scorching heat of the noon. My daydream got a jolt in a wailing. Koili's mother was dragging her on floor while beating her with a stick. The little naked child was following them crying continuously.

I did not know when I reached over there. The quiet neighbourhood resounded with the shouts of Koili's mother. She has been working as a daily labourer since two months in the construction site of my house.

I snatched the stick and said "Leave her...leave her.... are you going to kill this child or what ?"

"Yes, I shall kill her and suck her blood"

"What did you say? Look at my hand" I picked up a stick and was about to beat her. I was really angry. Just I cannot tolerate such uncivilised things.

Koili's mother left her daughter, threw the stick and said.

"Sir, you won't understand me. If she does drill for hours together every day-how can I manage? She is such a grown up girl- but she cannot bring a bundle of grass for the goat or collect dried droppings of the cow for fuel... she cannot even cook the rice properly. Come and see how she has burnt the rice. The eldest son is bed ridden for a month. Middle one is blind as such. God only knows for what sin he has become blind. And this girl is of no use for both sides. Her wretched father went to Calcutta to find another woman leaving all three creatures on my shoulder. More than that this girl is torturing me like anything."

Hearing all these I turned softer inside. But I was not

ready to express my emotion. Rather I said "Why don't you get her admitted in a school? Will she not be very wayward by sitting at home all alone ?

"Why should I enroll her name? Do you know whom have I not sent to the school? That wretched head mistress has sent them back while asking for this or that. The school fees are also so high otherwise I had a desire to educate my eldest son and make him a magistrate."

This time Koili's mother shrank her face helplessly. I would not help laughing at her last sentence, but somehow, I restrained myself.

"Are you talking of this girl sir ? Why should I educate her ? At her age I was married to her father. I was so busy in cooking for fifteen members, making cow dung-fuel, cleaning and scrubbing the house, gathering rice grain etc. that there was hardly any time left for myself. When did I do drill or pick up book and slate ?"

I was mixing the darkness of the past with the light of the present. My God ! I could only see two small glowing eyes of Koili in the frozen darkness all around.

"Look here Sir, these are broken chalks, slate, books etc. She is such an educated daughter of mine ! As if she would earn and support us. Are you not getting a pinch of poison ......what will you eat today.... just get lost...."

Koili's mother took out a piece of broken slate from the rags worn by Koili and threw at her in front of my eyes. She pulled up the torn cloth and taking the child in her arm she went almost like running. As if she does not care for the whole creation and its principles. The dark complexioned girl with bony frame in a torn pant almost reduced to a skeleton. She is standing before me in an unsecured position, as if she does not have faith in any one. There are red scratches of grass all over her body. She will be around twelve or thirteen years old. As if youth has forgotten her. Yet her mother has named her Koili (meaning Cuckoo). Koili was shedding tears looking at the torn and trampled book and broken slate. I was not able to speak out something that I thought to do. As in some situations man is overwhelmed with kindness and generosity, perhaps like that tears of kindness came to my eyes. Suddenly a loud call came piercing through the atmosphere "Hey Koili...... you wretch... beggar... are you coming soon or else I will see you..." I was startled. As if a strong wind took away page after page.... it came somewhere from a rough and cracking voice.

"Hey Rebi ! you wretch... you rogue !"

My body shivered in spite of the scorching heat of summer. I was standing dumbfounded putting fingers in the ears. Koili was running as fast as if she was struck by a stick. As if sharp and dazzling knife of heat could not touch her dark and thin body.

I could see the terror figure of Koili's mother from a distance. She is an ill-reputed quarrelsome woman for her zest for non-stop quarrelling in this locality. Nobody dares talking with her if it is not so necessary.

I stretched myself on bed while thinking of Koili. Rosy was sleeping in the next bed. Through my closed eyelids I was searching for Koili in Rosy After some time she would wake up and would get ready herself for her tutor and then in the evening she would go out to join Soni's birth-day party. For half of the days the programme is like this. And for this there are so much planning, preparation and busy engagements at home. But.... it is a useless thing... my concern for Koili is simply absurd. It is only a whim- a whim which I cannot sustain. Moreover, everybody would laugh it away thinking it as my luxury of imagination.

Next day the drum started beating again as it was Saturday. My sleep broke as if for the welcome of a much awaited moment. I stood near the railing keeping my mouth shut. The ayah had taken Rosy to the ground... because she did not like to do drill. But for the physical fitness especially for the body, which is brought up with more care, more protein, fat diet, there is no good medicine other than drill.

But I was not searching for Rosy. Rather I was searching for Koili. But she was not seen around. Perhaps she was sleeping due to severe pain of thrashing by her mother or she could not as her mother kept an eye on her at home. My heart shook with an unknown pain somewhere. The beauty and splendour, the brilliance of education of so beautiful girls glitter only in Koili's presence, with Koili as measuring standard. Otherwise, it is so ordinary.

Opening the window in the noon I looked at the playground and found no one. She won't come. Yet I am feeling restless... I won't be able to sleep or take rest. Unconsciously I reached near Koili's mother. Sitting under the shadow of the thatched roof of the open courtyard Koili's mother was doing Koili's hair with a wooden comb and was killing lice on her nail. And Koili ? She was scribbling something on a broken slate.... sometimes she was writing hastily looking at the pages of a torn book. And with that her head was shaking for which her mother slapped her harshly at her cheek. Somehow or other her mother made a plait and put a red coloured plastic butterfly on it. Then when she took some turmeric paste from a bowl and put it on her face, Koili cried. Her mother shouted, "you damned black ! I arranged turmeric and oil with so much difficulties and you don't like it. Where shall I get talcum powder for her ? I have lost sleep since two days for this marriage proposal and look at her. She is sitting with slate and chalk. That school has taught all these rubbish things....Hey are you like those girls ? Look, she is going to study! Listen, your father in law should not know all these things. Throw that slate and chalk away. You are after all a girl."

I shouted.

"Hey Koili's mother, are you going to get your daughter married ?"

"Sir ! when did you come ? Hey, what are you looking at ? Go and a get a mat"

"It's ok. I don't need it. Are you going to get Koili married?"

"Yes, it would take place if it were there in her fate. Today they would come to see her. So, I was giving her a makeup of oil and turmeric. There is nothing as such. Yet I also have self-respect. A rich family... two storehouses filled with rice ... the boy is too handsome like Lord Kartika .... Don't you know? Son of that driver Karuni- what is his name ? yes , Laxmana,"

My head reeled Laxman is more than 35 years old. More over his first wife is dead. His second wife has three children whom he has deserted since one year. So many times, Karuni has complained me that he is getting drunk and roaming here and there. He feels so harassed. And with that Laxmana a young girl like Koili...!

I thundered at her.

"How much money has he given to you ? Do you know if you do so the police would arrest you-the Govt. would put you behind the bar.... in the eyes of law ."

My words remained half-said. Koili's mother tightened the cloth around her waist and said-

"I warn you , don't tell anything at my face standing in my own house. I don't care for the police or the Govt. I shall do whatever I like to do with her , she is my daughter. Are you scaring me of Govt.? Is he blind ? There is nothing at home to eat, not a place to live in. When my husband deserted me leaving the four children with me, did I not then tell the police or the gentlemen of this locality ? Who came to feed my children? Look, my eldest son has been bedridden since a month. The medical staff did not keep him in the hospital. They refused to admit him. Even a handful of rice is not available in eight days. Let me know, where are these police and Govt? Yes, I am surviving today only because of that Laxman....whenever I ask for anything he will get it for me by any means. Look, he has given ten rupees in cash to buy things for marriage."

When Koili's mother started opening the knot made in the end of her saree, I could not stand there. In a way I ran away from there. The voice of Koili's mother was piercing at my back like a spear-" Oh, I am quite habituated with such fruitless concern and moral teaching-any fish that slips out of hand is always big."

After eight days I was getting ready to fly for Delhi in the evening. I was supposed to take Rosy and get her admitted in Loreto Convent, Delhi. It was time for plane I was worried thinking that I would leave Rosy in a far off place. Rosy stood near me in her pink dress and with full-fledged health. She looked like a fresh rose. When I embraced her with pain and emotional intensity someone entered house hurriedly. They were Koili and her mother. I looked at the turmeric coloured black body of Koili. She was having that red butterfly and wearing a red coloured cotton saree. There were bangles in both of her hands. Koili's mother said- "Go and touch master's feet. What are you gazing at blankly ? Sir, somehow or other the marriage ceremony is over ! I kept the groom for a day. I won't be able to do anymore. Today is wedding farewell. So, I brought her for your blessing."

Koili touched my feet bowing her head. I just looked at her face. Does she understand the meaning of marriage ? Does she understand the responsibility of family life ? Is she weeping because every girl does so ? I could not look at her face. In spite of all my strength my heart wept within while embracing Rosy.

Koili turned back. Something fell from her waist. When she bent down to collect it her mother put her feet on her hand and said "Fie on you ! You have lost all the grace of a girl. Are you not ashamed of taking chalk to your in law's place to study over there ? I should have been dead rather than seeing it. Koili could not take the chalk. Her mother pulled her hand forcefully and both left.

I did not have time. I closed the room hurriedly and went with Rosy.

x x x x x x x x x x x

After spending one month-holiday when I returned home in a blank mind, the sun was about to set. Looking at the sky of dusk- hour I was enveloped with a sense of loneliness.

Suddenly I met Koili's mother. She was staring at me blankly as if she could not recognize me - an unfamiliar person in an unknown land. The moment I stepped down from the car she put her arms round me tightly and said-

"Where did you leave didimoni ? Won't she run away ? How did you leave her alone? She would run away in the night .... get her drowned in the river... would hang herself or would take poison... poor fellow ! Why did you leave her.... Koili...Oye Koili.... you wretch ... you rogue."

I had never imagined such heart rending cry from

Koili's mother in her incoherent words. She was talking wildly while holding me tightly like that.

Rehman, my driver shouted-" You old rag ! leave him" Rehman, dragged her and made her sit on the verandah. Putting her face between the knee she started talking to herself. I was waiting to know the issue from Rehman.

"You left for Delhi on the wedding day of her daughter. Hardly eight days had passed her daughter ran away from home. Why should she run away sir ? Perhaps Laxman had murdered her in the drunken state and had buried her somewhere. We searched so many unknown places. But her dead body is not found yet. Some say she herself jumped into the river, some say she has taken poison, and for this her mother has lost mental balance. She is roaming round all through the night- she is scolding laughing and is calling her daughter's name is such a way that..."

I had neither patience nor courage nor even the necessity to hear anything more. I had also no interest to console Koili's mother. I was moving upstairs crossing step by step. There was emptiness and only emptiness, the empty home and empty earth.

I was dumb-struck when I opened the room. There were few pieces of chalk on my mosaic floor. Suddenly a gust of wind brought that wailing into the room. "Koili... Oye Koili... you wretch ... you rogue... where had you gone.... my queen... my dear... come... come my dear Koi... come.... come... I have got chalk and slate for you... come... come... come... Koi... come...!."

As if being haughty and moody she is perching on the branches of the tree or she is flying over the roof tops in the vast expanse of the sky- searching for a Spring !!!

The Auditorium

Prasanta himself does not know how he would forget the fact that he has come out of home in an angry mood. Standing under the croton tree in front of the canteen he was trembling in the scorching heat of imminent summer and was thinking that what would happen if he would walk out like a passerby who has forgotten his route ? Without going to office, he would be gone for ever...days and nights would have passed and like those months and years... Where would it have ended ? And where would he have stopped... there... there... there would be no one- and if so, there would be an old demon eating a tiger or a lion while putting her two legs in the fire. Something would have been there ! What is there beyond the horizon...

Thinking all this his mood became upset again. At first, he was feeling hurt because all were neglecting him thinking that he was a queer fellow. They were cutting jokes also. Even Susama, his wife had once written a letter to her sister in law complaining that they had tied her with a mad fellow. His father, mother, brother, friends and relatives and all have the same idea that Prasant is an idiosyncratic fellow. He has been laughed at with that. Again, when they need him, they would caress him like a pet cat. As if he were a strange human being who is back tired and exhausted after moving round desolate dense jungle. He never retreats in the commitment of giving everything.

Now it is painful for him. And with that pain inside he is unable to distinguish between good and bad, rules and misrule, anger and irritation. Now a days he tends to be reactive to ordinary and usual matter. He is deeply affected with the anguish of exercising his own self.

Today morning his father came from the garden and said, "Now that you have got promotion, send at least Rs.50/- to the Radhamadhab temple before giving treat to your friends and officers!".

It was more an order from a point of talking. He never had the tendency to understand and explain a point right from the beginning. How can he have it today ? The money is not so important even though it is the only standard of measurement of the entire world for his father. Following his father his mother also repeated same thing and caressing his back she made him conscious of his forgetfulness. He felt like breaking the house with his shouts. But he could not do so.

At last Susama roared into a long laughter while drying her wet hair with a towel and said " Did you remember it or not? You may not listen to me, but you should obey your parents......" It is not that her words lack irony. But Prasanta felt that it is simply useless to argue with this foolish woman and within half an hour he went out after getting dressed and usually doing his hair just casually. Like this he has come out so many times saying that he has engagements with his friends or has urgent work in the office or he is not feeling well and so on.... He has wandered the whole day without food.... as if sometimes one feels good by torturing himself. Again, he has returned home in the evening, has taken tea and snacks sitting on the verandah, has played with his son, has gone to temple with mother or has gone to cinema with Susama. As if someone from above is holding the rein of doll-show and is making him dance accordingly to the tune.

No, he does not like it anymore, he cannot compromise anymore. Family ...friends, relatives, society, country and the world, all are terribly disgusting. He does not have the guts to go somewhere and sit peacefully for a moment with someone. All are busy in telling their own problems. Who is listening to whom ? Where is time ? Where is energy ? Where is also the heart ?

That day Prasanta had asked Atasi about her daily life and how she is pulling on etc. She replied with a smile and said that it goes like all other's. If there might be an exception in single life ! Many times, Atasi had told her that everything is same in the process of time. Hardly there is a difference between whim and belief or realization. Yet he has seen Atasi overwhelmed with happiness and pleasures. He has seen her stopping round the market for saree and ornaments, prostrating before God for hours together in the temple. He has also heard that... Atasi used to go to club and takes alcohol there. When this rumour spread over the entire office then Prasanta asked about it. Atasi laughed carelessly and said-

"Prasanta ! you have a mad-quest for everything. But... I do not like to get involved like you. All this is an experiment. You may call it madness or perversion. But that understanding should be right... otherwise it is so difficult... !"

Prasanta never understands Atasi. Like so he does not understand many others. He wonders when he would think of his intimate friend Ashis. Even getting less salary than him and maintaining a joint family he has made a home and car and is lost himself in the bliss of complete life. Whenever he meets him, he would repeat the same thing- "Can you lend some money, Prasanta ? If I don't buy a refrigerator for my sister's marriage then I won't manage it later in such price-hike."

Since two months he has been arranging money for refrigerator. Before it was for house, car and ornaments etc. That is his only problems, the only thing, the only addiction, addiction for money- he is mad after that addiction. So, Prasanta would feel tired when he goes to him... it is not because of his inability, but for his unwillingness and disgust to tell him his own problem !

And the known and unknown faces he used to meet and talk to in the interval of cinema, marriage party or other celebrations, the only point of conversation of the whole crowd, the only concern, the only dream for future- how much salary will increase, how much price will come down for rice and oil, how long the Government would last ? As a high official he has answered these many times like an all unknowing one and sometimes he has avoided it in a very casual manner. There is no way out. He does not dare of doing something on his part other than getting swept in an unknown flow. He is breaking within because whenever he tries to solve the problem, he would at last reach the original point after roaming all over. As if every day someone is holding a machine and is sowing seeds of problems and sufferings on human breast and all are getting into the wheel and are running after helplessly grasping the circle of the wheel. No one has courage to leave it and come out. Fear ? Fear for what ? For life or for death ? Leaving aside these two things there is not the third one for which man would plan, dream.... !

Nay, Prasanta would start declaring war against this world. Where there is no life, no heart, no understanding, no peace or happiness, what credit it serves for getting dragged for living over there ? He would tell this and walk out. Let all know, atleast one man has gone with a protest and he would also know it.... !

As if someone has roared into laughter and said- Mad fellow ! The world knows that millions of people like this have gone out of her reach in every age since time immemorial. Whom have they taken with them ? And how many steps ? In spite of having this experience and without having the intellect of great man, does this insignificant Prasanta want to go out ? Let him go if he wants so. Who bothers for that ? It won't mark even a coma on the pages of history with his protest call.

Would Prasanta then go quietly ? He would walk out without informing father-mother, son-daughter, Susama, office-service, promotion, friends, relatives. Does his personality not have any value ?

In his helpless condition, the sadness was spreading over his each cell with a sense of growing intolerance in Prasanta. As if he has reached a point like top-knot. With a little more of meld wild it would roll down far, too far, miles and miles away, nobody would know its existence, even he himself. If he lets this moment passed, Prasanta would lag behind he won't be able to go. In every age each successful man can become great only with the advantage of chance. One can cross the circle of time through an ordinary stop. He knows this. No more delay. No waiting for anyone- neither the expectation of assurance nor of possession... Now he would go.

One... two-

"Hey Prasanta ! My God ! I have been searching you like anything. And you are here"

As if suddenly someone had cut down the two extending arms of Prasanta into pieces with an axe of words.

Who? His father. One who has given him birth physically and one who is proud of making him a specimen-like human being by giving his own share of pleasure and money- it is his father.

In the unspeakable pain of his slain arms tears rolled down from Prasanta's eyes and silently like that he started the marathon race once again hanging down his extending arms. Again, he raised his left and right legs and started one... two ...

"My God ! Why are you looking at him like this ? Just see... see. If his limbs are having epileptic strokes. We can pay the rickshaw fare later...!"

It is his mother. Gone case. Susama and his son must have also come here searching for him. What is the reason ? Promotion, service, future security.

Someone dragged his two legs back before he says 'three.' Then followed few other big and small palms ! As it were the earth's. All the big and small forces were detaching his head, legs, hands from his body. They were taking the share as per their needs.

When he tried to free the two legs with all his force and failed and cried out in pain, he felt that someone was hammering his head... words and voices were piercing his ears like spears !

"We have to lift him... yes... take care... slowly... he is senseless ...."

"Since few days he would remain standing under the sun... would not respond to our call ... that croton tree is very old... God knows... you people do not believe anything."

"Since three days my son has not taken his meal... has forgotten hunger and thirst. But does my daughter in law tell me something about it ? ...... How do I come to know...."

"Please get side yourself. We would take him to the

hospital by car. I think there is nothing serious... but he seems ill since few days. Any way Mr. Mohapatra, you should be careful – of course I am trying to arrange two months leave for him !"

"Sir, would it create any trouble for promotion or salary ?"

After this Prasanta could not hear anything except Susama's sobbing and murmurs of few unintelligible words. His breath was choking with unbearable pain near the neck ! As if someone is cutting his throat from his body slowly with the edge of a saw ! He could not open his lips even if he tried so much.

It is also good in one way. No one would listen to him if he says something without having head, hands and legs ? Yet ! Yet the world knows that there would be no more delay for the birth of another world !!

The Twins

Now as if he did not remember anything ! What was he talking about ! Actually, where did the talk start and where did it end and where was he in the next moment, he had not understood yet.

Niranjan shook him and said- "Hey Naresh, it is left half said ! It is interesting to hear. Let us talk. But I cannot recollect and say anything like you. You know, I can never recollect my childhood days. I have always stayed away from home. If I had stayed with my parents...!"

Naresh could not hear what Niranjan was saying after wards. The image of a tearful woman leaning against the wall of a far-off village who never opened the mouth in spite of thousands of accusations and torture on her floated before his eyes. There was no flesh on her white skinned body. The whole twenty four hours of the day she was busy with household chorus. Her face was wearing the same expression in the moment of joy at home and also in the moment of crisis or any emergency- one that is seen at the climax point of suffering, never gets back again. Naresh felt that he had seen her eye to eye. 'Oh'- the sound came out in suffering and pain.

Niranjan held Naresh and said – "Did you get hurt somewhere? What happened ? That is a stoney road. I tell you to go on the other way. But you are not ready to listen......"

"No, nothing has happened. Suddenly my mother came into my mind. Niranjan, perhaps you won't believe that I can never recollect her face. In our childhood days she was so busy with her household works that hardly we have met her. Suppose we meet, she would not talk and we also would be in a position to listen. When I was getting ready to fly for London, the last time I had seen her standing and looking through the window while leaning against the wall. That's all. Seeing me there were tears in her eyes. But she said nothing. I would not say good bye to her also. That means...!"

"Yes, what happened after that ? That means Naresh, have you ever gone to see your mother after returning from London ?"

"No, there was not even time, I could not get time to think over."

Niranjan sat on the stone and said "Hey Naresh ! sit, please sit. Let us discuss the matter. After staying five years in London and back here again you have spent forty-five years, yet you do remember today only and that too at an odd moment when it should never come to mind. How strange are you ?"

It rained few drops. The cold and pale moon was hidden by the patches of clouds. The head was reeling. I could not recollect anything of what I was saying or thinking. I could not see my face nor I could recollect the questions put by Niranjan.

"Why are you not sitting ? Sit for a while, tell me more about your mother. It feels good to hear it."

Naresh got irritated and said.

"You don't have a little commonsense. Do you know what is the time of night ? Another two miles left to go. It may rain now.......... you started your romance on the way only asking me to tell this and that. But you yourself won't say anything."

Niranjan knew that Naresh had consumed over dose of alcohol today. Along with intoxicant abnormality there is a sign of forgetfulness. Turning the direction of discussion he said-

"Well ! will you hear from me ? Then I can talk about Suma, means about Susama – the romantic story of first love."

"Shut up Niranjan ! I don't have patience to hear anything. And at the late hour of night when your wife would be waiting for you at home, what is the case of churning the memory of first love ? There are very few people on earth who have turned successful in their first love. The man has to live with the second a third while thinking about the first one throughout his life. Son, daughter, wife, profession all are illusion only. But it is strange that man never gets rid of that inspite of his innumerable efforts. Why should you put that a question today ?"

Naresh was sweating as he said all these things in one breath and taking the handkerchief from the pocket, he stated fanning himself.

Niranjan got angry and said –

"Do you understand ! why are you so intolerant ? Have you ever thought of anyone other than your own problems ? You don't even have the patience to hear a word from someone else. Yet...."

Naresh asked in a suppressed voice-

"What yet ? You tell whatever you like. Why did you stop? Nobody loves unconditionally on earth, that I know. How could you be an exception from this ?

The floating clouds scattered few more big drops of water. As if the jungle had caught fire and its burning flame subsided with it. Niranjan became embarrassed and got up.

Both friends looked at each other silently. What sort of self-analysis is it at the last stage of old age. Is it an attempt of a mad elephant to demolish a beautifully decorated flower-gate ?

Holding Naresh's hands Niranjan said-

"Naresh, let's go. It is quite late and I am feeling tired. Annapurna would be waiting for you."

"And for you ? There is no one to wait."

A complaining mood was found clearly in Naresh's tone. Niranjan smiled drily and said-

"No ! In the strict sense of the term, it is not waiting. Take for example, somebody would be waiting at the gate simply to lock the gate after I entered the house."

"And Bimla ? Has she gone to sleep?"

"Ah ! What are you saying Naresh ! Does it mean waiting if somebody would simply stare and sit near the kitchen after finishing cooking.?"

"What do you mean by it ? What sort of distorted thoughts at this age ?"

"Leave it, leave it ! Naresh, you won't be able to understand. If you had understood, then you would not have thought of your mother at the last point of a fulfilled life. Of-course in that respect you are happy. I don't remember my mother's face at all."

"But you can remember Susama's face."

"That is why I can understand the pain of your inability to see mother, perhaps at one stage."

Naresh interrupted and said –"both are same"

It started drizzling and rained heavily. Nobody marked when clouds spread over the entire sky. There was intense smell of wet earth all around and gulmohor trees on both sides. Whether the moon was hidden in the wind in the rain, nobody knew ! Holding each other's hand the two friends started running ahead. No! it was impossible to go. Both of them stood under a tree nearby. Their palms were only trembling terribly.

It was a heavy down pour of rain. The street looked desolate. The street light was blinking. As if there was no one in this world. Is the earth born of a dark hole? Where do they exist ? Are they the twins of first creation ? How strange ? Where does the road lead to ?

Looking at Niranjan Naresh said –

"You had a bad habit in our student days. You tend to slip your hand or taking advantage of others' absent mindedness you disappear somewhere. Hope, you won't repeat it again in such a raining night."

While breaking into childish laughter Niranjan stopped and pointing at the speed of a flying bird in the sky he said-

"Look, Naresh, look ! An awaiting-bird is flying. Ah! How has it waited for rain ! I do not really understand what life is ... whether it is a vast question of who, what and why or a combination of unending experiences. There is pleasure... also pain...!"

"See Niranjan ! Do not begin an introduction and more over to your first love Suma alias Susama. I am thick tired of hearing that epic.... The conclusion i.e., Susama's death is left only. Would death have left her only because she was your lady love ?"

"How strange ! Do you have such a low opinion of me ? If you think that I want to interfere in the rules and regulation of the world, then you have done utmost injustice to me. I do not want immortality for me." By that time Niranjan's voice was broken with sadness.

Naresh thought of something and said-

"I do not understand where your pain and suffering lie. Because you cannot marry her....

"No, No ! Susama had never expected anything from me throughout the life. She wanted only an assurance from me."

"What ? What is that promise that has made her distinct from other women and other love ?" Naresh asked irritatingly.

Niranjan said –

"He wished that whenever she calls me. I would reach there. I had also assured her."

"How many times had she called ? As if I don't know. You never stay at home during any vacation. Moving anywhere even without informing Bindu...."

"See, Naresh ! I have told you earlier that you won't be able to understand Susama. She has expected nothing from me. Not even a minute of my time. My vacation, leisure was spent in other places, business, gambling and clubs.... if Susama did not want it was impossible for me to go to her yet her 'wish' is just like the pain of the peacock waiting for rainwater."

Naresh gave a break and said-

"Then, when and how many times has she called you? And what did she ask for ?"

"I would have been happy if I had given her something. I would have less repentance today."

"Leave it ! She called, you went, she asked nothing, you did not give or did not get a scope to give. Died ?"

"No, she cannot die. One who does not have a beginning, how can she have an end ? And who is the artist or painter on earth who can say the last word ? Moreover, I am not God."

Naresh did not know what to do. As if all of a sudden everything was scattered. As if the fury of rain soaked wind made his shirt torn and was hanging him at the doorstep of an eternal vaccume.

Niranjan broke the silence and said-

"Naresh, let's to. It is too late now. The rain has stopped. I am feeling tired."

"No ! you tell me the last part; else I won't go. Tell me when Susama called you and what did she say then ?"

Niranjan shouted-

"What is this, Naresh? Don't you have a heart ? Don't you understand ?

"No, no, I cannot understand. You will have to tell."

"Then listen. I never had that last meeting with her. That means she never called me till she took leave of this world ! But she had written to me. Love is an eternal waiting.......... that has no suffering, no sadness and no question of getting it. So, I would not make it narrow by taking advantage of a particular time......... cruel, the cruel woman. Even with this you don't understand......"

Naresh put his two palms on his face and said in an anguished tone-"Niranjan ! I do not understand why I am feeling so restless today suddenly thinking of my mother. I wish I could sleep once like a child on her lap...."

Niranjan did not say anything. He had no time or scope to express his grief.

Suddenly a number of little birds started chirping at a time in a tree. A bird flew over the sky opening its wide wings.... The rain ceased. The roads looked clear and fresh.

Each streamlet of the rain does not touch the lips of the rain-bird nor does the spring wind fill each neem tree with the sandalwood fragrance.

The moment never returns again. If at all it returns,

it does not have the first colour and sweetness. Niranjan knows this truth well that repetition spoils the speciality of a moment. So, with what sorrow would he call himself a destitute ? In riches and luxury, he is far more powerful than Naresh or even any other man.

Embracing Naresh with intense emotion Niranjan said...

"Come. It is too late now. We may not wait for anyone.... but many wait for us. Come, it is getting late..."

Black Eagle Books

www.blackeaglebooks.org
info@blackeaglebooks.org

Black Eagle Books, an independent publisher, was founded
as a nonprofit organization in April, 2019. It is our mission
to connect and engage the Indian diaspora and the world at
large with the best of works of world literature published on
a collaborative platform, with special emphasis on
foregrounding Contemporary Classics and New Writing.